THE THRONE
HE MUST TAKE

THE THRONE HE MUST TAKE

BY

CHANTELLE SHAW

First published in Great Britain 2017
By Mills & Boon, an imprint of HarperCollins*Publishers*
1 London Bridge Street, London, SE1 9GF

Large Print edition 2018

© 2017 Chantelle Shaw

ISBN: 978-0-263-07326-3

MIX
Paper from
responsible sources
FSC
www.fsc.org   FSC® C007454

This book is produced from independently certified FSC™ paper to ensure responsible forest management. For more information visit www.harpercollins.co.uk/green.

Printed and bound in Great Britain
by CPI Group (UK) Ltd, Croydon, CR0 4YY

CHAPTER ONE

What did *happen to Vostov's royal children?*

THE NEWSPAPER HEADLINE caught Holly Maitland's eye when she walked into the reception lounge of the Frieden Clinic to await the arrival of her new client.

The exclusive private psychiatric practice catered for an international clientele, and like most of the clinic's staff Holly was fluent in several languages. She noted that the French, Italian and German newspapers all bore similar headlines to the English papers. But until the recent media interest in Vostov she—and, she suspected, many other people—had never heard of the tiny principality in the Balkans.

She turned her attention away from the newspapers, which were neatly arranged on a coffee table in front of an elegant brocade sofa. Large windows on three sides of the room offered spectacular views of the Austrian Alps. The gentle tick of an antique wall clock barely intruded on the cloistered quiet of the lounge, and the general ambience was one of discreet luxury.

Outside, the mountains stood guard like a craggy fortress, with their sharp peaks pointing towards a topaz-blue sky. Last night's fresh snowfall glistened in the winter sunshine.

Holly scrutinised the road that snaked its way up from Salzburg. The snow-clearing machines had already done their job, but there were no cars on the road and her client was late.

She felt a flicker of irritation as she wondered why he had declined to be collected from the airport by a chauffeur and driven to the Frieden Clinic which was the usual arrangement. She hoped he was not going to be difficult, but all the indications suggested that Jarek Dvorska Saunderson was likely to be a pain in someone's backside. *Hers.*

Jarek was a high-flier in the City of London, often described as 'the man with the Midas touch' after his success on the stockmarket which had earned him a personal multi-million-pound fortune. But a couple of years ago there had been problems at Saunderson's Bank—one of the UK's most prestigious private banks—where Jarek had held a senior position. He had been fired by the bank's new chairman, who also happened to be his brother-in-law: Spanish business tycoon Cortez Ramos.

The blip in his career had evidently not impacted on Jarek's jet-set lifestyle. He was pursued relentlessly by the paparazzi, and rarely did a week pass without another exposé in the tabloids of his outrageous exploits—usually accompanied by a photo of him with a blonde bimbo draped around him.

Stories of his heavy drinking, partying and womanising were legendary—as was his passion for the risky sport of motorbike racing. There had been intense news coverage recently, when he had crashed his bike during a race and afterwards assaulted a journalist who had tried to interview him. It was that event which had apparently prompted Jarek to seek help for his 'issues', Professor Franz Heppel, the medical director of the Frieden Clinic, had explained to Holly during a briefing about her new patient.

She glanced at the clock. Maybe he wasn't coming? She knew only too well how hard it was to face up to personal demons, and from the sound of it Jarek Saunderson had his fair share of those.

A rumbling noise jolted her from her thoughts and she instinctively looked up at the higher slopes of the mountains. During the winter months the avalanche risk in the Alps was high, particularly after heavy snowfall. But there was no sign of the kind of fast-moving white mass that struck fear into the hearts of skiers and climbers. She looked back at the road as the throaty, roaring noise grew louder and saw a motorbike hurtling around the bends.

Minutes later Holly watched the bike turn onto the private road leading to the Frieden Clinic and wondered if the rider was her client. It would be typical of everything she'd heard about Jarek for him to ride a motorbike into the mountains in January, when there was the threat of treacherous black ice on the roads. A sports commentator who had watched him compete in the notoriously dangerous Isle of Man TT superbike race had suggested that either Jarek had a death wish or a massive ego which made him believe he was indestructible.

Her first assignment at the Frieden Clinic

promised to be interesting, possibly challenging, and ultimately—she hoped—successful, Holly mused. She was keen to make a good impression with Professor Heppel during the three-month probation period of her new job. His world-renowned clinic employed the very best international experts, and her appointment as a psychotherapist was a huge boost to her career.

The noise of the motorbike stopped, and from her vantage point at the window she watched the rider dismount. As she passed the mirror in the entrance hall she glanced at her reflection, to check that her hair was neatly secured in its chignon. Her crisp white blouse, navy skirt and low-heeled black shoes were businesslike, although she noted with a grimace that the blouse gaped slightly across her bust. A result of too many helpings of the chef's *apfelstrudel*, she thought ruefully.

It occurred to her that Stuart would not have approved of her more voluptuous shape. When she had shown him pictures of herself as a nineteen-year-old photographic model he had raved about her slim figure, even though she had clearly been unhealthily thin.

'My modelling career was ten years ago and I survived on a diet of apples and black coffee,' she'd told him when he'd nagged her to go to the gym. 'Women were designed to have breasts and hips, and I have no intention of starving myself to conform to the fashion industry's unrealistic ideal of how women should look.'

A few months after that conversation Stuart had dumped her and announced his engagement to willowy blonde Leanne, who was now pregnant with his baby.

Holly swiftly shut off the painful thought as she opened the door and stepped outside to the porch to welcome her patient. She had moved from London to Austria two weeks ago, and loved living in the mountains where the air was fresh and clean. But the smell of cigarette smoke drifting towards her now made her wrinkle her nose in disgust.

'Mr Saunderson?' The man had his back to her, but she was sure it was him. He had removed his crash helmet and the streaked blond hair spilling over the collar of his black leather jacket was recognisable from his too-numerous-to-count appearances in the tabloids. 'May I remind you that there is a strict no smoking policy at the Frieden Clinic? The house rules *are* listed in the brochure.'

The broad leather-clad shoulders lifted in a nonchalant shrug. 'I didn't read the brochure.'

Holly stifled the urge to knock the cigarette from his fingers and said tartly, 'What a pity. If you had, you would have seen that the Frieden Clinic takes a holistic approach to treating nicotine addiction and has an excellent success rate for helping to break a dependency on cigarettes.'

'I don't have a nicotine addiction.' He turned around then, and took another drag on his cigarette. 'You wouldn't begrudge the condemned prisoner a final cigarette, would you?'

He spoke in a lazy drawl and his mouth crooked into a careless smile as if he was well aware of his devastating effect on susceptible females.

'Smoking is a filthy habit,' Holly snapped, forgetting that she should take care not to reveal her personal prejudices. But her first sight of Jarek in the flesh, rather than in a photo in a newspaper, had made her forget everything. If he asked her name she would be unable to tell him, because the single thought in her head was that he was lethally attractive.

'Not as filthy as some of my other habits,' he murmured.

There was amusement in his voice, and a mocking gleam in eyes that even from a distance of a few feet away were like brilliant blue laser beams directed straight at Holly. She watched him grind the cigarette out against the sole of his boot and drop the stub into his pocket before he walked up the steps to join her on the porch.

While she groped for her sanity, and for something—anything—to say, his smile faded and there was a hard edge to his voice when he spoke again. 'And I no longer use my English adoptive parents' name: Saunderson. I prefer to be known by the name I was given at bir—' He stopped abruptly and then said, 'By my Bosnian name: Dvorska.'

'Right... Mr Dvorska. Um...' God, was that breathless voice really hers? Holly cleared her throat. 'Welcome to the Frieden Clinic.' She frowned as she recalled his comment. 'Why did you call yourself a condemned prisoner? Frieden is the German word for peace, and the Frieden Clinic is a place of sanctuary—not a prison. I hope you will find a sense of peace and tranquillity here, while I endeavour to help you on your journey to a lasting recovery from the emotional issues that have created a negative impact on your life.'

'Peace?' His laugh was an oddly grim sound. 'I sincerely doubt I'll ever find *that*. You say that *you* will be helping me on this wondrous journey to enlightenment?' His tone was sardonic. 'I'd assumed you are the receptionist. When I met Professor Heppel in London he told me I had been assigned a psychotherapist called Dr Maitland.'

'Forgive me. I should have introduced myself.' Feeling flustered, Holly extended her hand towards him. 'I'm Dr Holly Maitland.'

Almost imperceptibly Jarek Dvorska's demeanour changed. He still spoke in that lazy drawl, as if he was bored with his life—which, according to the gossip columns, was an endless round of parties with his similarly louche millionaire friends—but his ice-blue eyes were sharply intelligent and his intent gaze gave Holly the unsettling idea that he could see inside her head.

'You are *not* what I was expecting,' he murmured after a lengthy pause.

She swallowed as he enclosed her hand in a firm grasp. Heat shot up her arm, as if she'd stuck her fingers into an electrical socket, causing the tiny hairs on her skin to prickle. Far more embarrassingly, she felt her nipples tighten. Jarek dropped his gaze to her breasts and the eyes that had reminded Holly of glacial pools now gleamed hotly with a wicked promise that she assured herself had no effect on her.

'It's quite common to form ideas about another person before actually meeting them.' She ignored the frantic thud of her heart and gave him a cool smile. 'What were your expectations of me?'

'I assumed you would be older,' he said bluntly. 'Frankly I'm not interested in unburdening my soul to a psychologist. I'm only here because my sister believes I need to learn to control my temper, and my brother-in-law threatened to kill me if I do anything to upset Elin in the final weeks of her pregnancy.'

He did not sound as if he was joking.

Holly felt a pang of envy for Jarek's sister. She'd had many years to come to terms with her infertility, but there was still a little ache inside her when she heard of other women who were on the magical journey to motherhood.

She switched her thoughts to Jarek. There had been deep affection in his voice when he'd mentioned his sister, which belied his image in the tabloids of a reckless playboy who cared only about his personal gratification with an endless supply of pretty women.

'I suppose your reference to my age means you think I lack experience? But I can assure you I have a Doctorate in Counselling Psychology and Psychotherapy and I have experience working as a psychotherapist in both the private health sector and the NHS in England.'

The leather-clad shoulders lifted in another shrug that made Holly appreciate Jarek's formidable physique. She was slightly below average height, which was why she had never made it onto the catwalk during her brief modelling career, and he towered over her. She estimated he must be two or three inches over six feet tall.

'I don't doubt you are highly qualified,' he murmured. 'Professor Heppel spoke very highly of you. But he failed to mention that you are beautiful, Dr Maitland.'

It was not difficult to understand why women fell for him in droves. He could turn on his charm as easily as flicking a switch. His husky voice smouldered with a sensual heat that made her insides melt and it took all her willpower to meet his gaze calmly.

'Professor Heppel offered me a job at his clinic based on my reputation as a dedicated psychotherapist,' she said crisply. 'Please—call me Holly,' she continued. 'We are going to be spending a lot of time together over the next few weeks and we need to feel comfortable around each other. It is important to establish trust and respect between a patient and his therapist.'

'Comfortable...' Jarek rolled the word off his tongue in a smoky, sexy voice that lit a flame in the pit of Holly's stomach. 'Women don't usually feel *comfortable* around me. My talents are considerable...' he grinned at her startled expression '...but offering comfort is not one of them.'

'I don't suppose it is,' she said drily. 'I'm sure your legions of female devotees are attracted to your dangerous image. But presumably your numerous shallow affairs fail to make you happy? Which is why you have sought the help of a psychotherapist to enable you to make changes in your lifestyle that will allow you to have more fulfilling relationships.'

'I told you—I've only agreed to undergo therapy to please my sister.'

His lazy smile did not change but the warmth had gone from his eyes, leaving them as cold and hard as ice. Holly gave a little shiver. There was something predatory about him that was at variance with his reputation of a dissolute playboy. She had a feeling that people saw in Jarek exactly what he wanted them to see. But if the life that he played out in the full glare of the media was a lie, who was the *real* Jarek Dvorska?

'Why do women think that men can only feel fulfilled if they are in a relationship?' he drawled. 'I'm perfectly content to have shallow affairs— in fact the shallower the better. The truth is that the ultimate male fantasy is for hot, hard sex without strings. Emotional strings, I mean. *Real* strings add an interesting element to sex play, but personally I prefer to use silk cords for bondage games.'

Holly was furious with herself for blushing—and furious with him for being an arrogant jerk. To think she'd wasted thirty seconds of her life wondering if he had hidden depths! But, like it or not—like *him* or not—Jarek was her client and it was vital that she established a rapport with him. At the end of his six-week stay at the clinic he would discuss with Professor Heppel if her treatment had been successful for him. A bad report would jeopardise her job at the Frieden Clinic—but, more than that, psychotherapy was her vocation, and she had a genuine desire to help every patient she worked with.

She made herself smile at Jarek. 'We can explore your theories about relationships and the possible reasons for your fear of commitment during our sessions. It's good that you can speak openly and honestly regarding your feelings about casual sex. You can be confident that I will do my best to help you with your issues.'

He threw back his head and laughed—low and husky and outrageously sensual. 'I promise you I don't need any help with sex, angel-face.'

Holly knew she was blushing again, and felt even more mortified when she saw Jarek's eyes flick down to her breasts again. He could hardly fail to notice the hard peaks of her nipples outlined beneath her blouse. 'Let's go inside, where it's warm,' she said tightly. 'I should have put my coat on before I came out to meet you and I'm cold,' she added, keen to emphasise that her body's involuntary reaction was to the icy temperature, and she was *not* affected by his potent masculinity.

Avoiding the speculative gleam in his eyes, she ushered him into the clinic and indicated a door leading off the entrance hall.

'Through there is a boot room, where ski equipment is kept and where you can leave your bike gear. Your luggage arrived this morning, and one of the support staff will take your cases to your private residential retreat later. I'll wait for you in the lounge. Would you like a cup of coffee?'

'I'd love one. I'm glad you don't disapprove of *all* stimulants. I was worried I'd have to give up every source of pleasure during my stay.'

His wicked grin did peculiar things to Holly's insides. She waited until he had closed the boot room door behind him before she released her breath. While she switched on the coffee percolator and arranged the cups on a tray she tried to rationalise why she had reacted to Jarek the way she had. Her heart was still beating too fast and every nerve-ending in her body felt acutely sensitive, so that she was aware of the scrape of her lace-edged bra against her breasts.

She hadn't expected him to be so *overwhelming*, she thought ruefully. Dressed in all that black leather, he'd exuded a primitive sensuality that had made her want… She bit her lip as a shocking image flashed into her mind of her lying naked on a bed, with her wrists secured to the headboard by silken cords. In her fantasy Jarek stroked his hands over her breasts and hips before he pushed her legs apart and bent his head to flick his tongue over the inside of her thighs.

'Careful.'

The smoky voice close to her ear jerked her from her erotic daydream and she looked down and saw that she had overfilled a cup and coffee was pouring over the rim into the saucer.

'Oh.' She hadn't heard him walk across the lounge and she dared not look at him, terrified that his laser-bright gaze might see inside her head. 'I'm terribly clumsy,' she gabbled as she

grabbed a handful of napkins and mopped up the spillage. 'How do you take your coffee?'

'Black and bitter—like my heart.'

Beneath his light tone there was something darker that made her wonder again who was the *real* Jarek? The jester, or the man with secrets that he seemed determined to keep hidden?

She handed him his coffee before adding cream and sugar to her own cup, craving a sweet fix to calm her nervous tension. Jarek sat down on the sofa. The empty space next to him was the obvious place for Holly to sit, but instead she chose an armchair. Only when she was at a safe distance from him did she look directly at him, and her heart gave an annoying jolt.

So much for her hope that without his biker leathers he would be less impressive. Superbly tailored black trousers drew her attention to his lean hips and the long legs that he thrust out in front of him. A charcoal-grey fine wool sweater moulded the hard ridges of his pectoral and abdominal muscles. His eyes were that astonishing bright blue, set in an angular face that was cruelly beautiful. He reminded her of a wolf—

especially when he flashed a wide grin that revealed his white teeth.

Holly forced herself to study him objectively. His cheekbones were too sharp and his mouth too wide for him to be conventionally handsome. She estimated that there was at least two days' growth of stubble on his square jaw, and his rakish appearance was accentuated by the streaked blond hair that hung down on either side of his face. He pushed it back with a careless sweep of his hand.

Needing an excuse to avoid looking at him, she jumped up and walked over to the sideboard where the clinic's presentation packs were kept.

'I'll explain a little bit about the aims of the Frieden Clinic and give you another brochure so that you can read our mission statement in full.'

She spoke to him over her shoulder.

'In a nutshell, our ethos is to identify and treat the root cause of each patient's problems. The problems which may have led them to become reliant on potentially harmful substances or exhibit particular behaviour traits. At the Frieden Clinic we understand that every patient is unique, and we tailor an individual programme of treatment and support, matching the patient with a psychologist who will live at an Alpine retreat with them and provide therapy whenever the patient requires it, twenty-four hours a day. As well as clinical therapy, patients are encouraged to experience the wide range of complementary therapies which are available, such as massage and yoga. Leisure time is another important aspect of your stay with us, and there will be opportunities for you to ski and to enjoy many other activities in the beautiful surroundings of the Austrian Alps.'

Having located the brochures in the last drawer she looked in, Holly turned to face Jarek and discovered that he had picked up a newspaper and was reading it. Evidently he was more interested in the story on the front page than what she had to say, she thought, annoyed by his rudeness.

'Would you like me to repeat any of what I've just told you?' she asked, in a painfully polite voice that failed to disguise the bite in her tone.

He dropped the newspaper onto the table and for a split second she glimpsed a...a *tortured* expression in his eyes. There was no other word to describe it. But then he blinked and Holly told herself she must have been imagining things, for his ice-blue gaze was indefinable.

'It all seems clear enough. If I'm a good boy I'll be allowed to go skiing,' he drawled.

He was her patient, and she would do her best to build a rapport with him even if it killed her, Holly told herself.

Through the window she saw a car draw up in front of the clinic.

'Your personal chauffeur, Gunther, is here to take you to Chalet Soline. You have also been assigned a gourmet chef, and a maid who will take care of you during your stay. Professor Heppel will visit you this evening, after you have had a chance to settle in. Several social events have been arranged for your enjoyment, including an evening in Salzburg which will be an opportunity for you to meet the rest of the medical team and other patients who are receiving treatment. Part of the evening's entertainment will be a chamber concert at the famous Marble Hall at the Mirabell Palace.'

'I'm not sure I'll be able to handle that amount of excitement,' he said drily. 'I hope there will be a well-stocked bar.'

'Clients are asked to abstain from alcohol whilst they are on a treatment programme,' Holly reminded him. 'But don't worry—I will be with you to support and encourage you on your journey to sobriety.'

Jarek got up from the sofa and the lounge suddenly seemed to shrink. It wasn't just his height that made him dominate the room. He exuded a raw magnetism that sent heat coursing through Holly's veins when he raked his bright blue eyes over her, from her head down to her toes, lingering a fraction longer than was appropriate on the firm swell of her breasts.

'I should have guessed from your schoolmarm appearance that you are a fan of chamber music. I bet your idea of an exciting night is to go to bed early with a milky drink,' he said, in that lazy, mocking way that made her want to slap him. *Hard.*

'My bedtime habits are not up for discussion,' she snapped, stung by his unflattering description of her. 'Schoolmarm' made her sound like a frump.

He was testing her professionalism to its limits. She had never met such an *infuriating* man.

She watched the corners of his mouth lift in a slow smile, as if he could not be bothered to exert more than the minimum of effort.

'We could discuss *my* bedtime habits instead, if you like? I guarantee they are more interesting and…energetic than yours.'

'I'm well aware of that. Anyone who reads the gutter press is regularly treated to intimate details about your love affairs.'

His grin widened, and his eyes had a wicked glint that made Holly's heart beat faster. How could his eyes be as cold as ice one minute and in the next instant burn with blue flames that made her feel hot all over?

'Presumably *you* read the tabloids, as you seem to know so much about me,' he said softly. 'The intimate details you mention are fifty per cent true and fifty per cent the product of an editor's fevered imagination. But I don't have *love* affairs.' His tone hardened. '*Love* plays no part in my sexual adventures. As long as you remember that, we should get on fine.'

'Why do I need to remember it? I'm not interested in your sex-life except in my professional capacity as your therapist.'

'Of *course* you're interested in me, angel-face. Those big brown eyes of yours soften like molten chocolate every time you look at me. Do you think I haven't noticed the hungry glances you've been darting at me when you think my attention's not on you?'

His smoky, sensual voice sent a shiver of unwanted reaction the length of Holly's spine. It was imperative that she took back control of the situation and of herself. Her reaction to Jarek was utterly inexplicable. He was an arrogant, oversexed playboy and the absolute anathema of the intellectual men she had dated in the past.

Before she'd left London she'd had dinner a couple of times with Malcom, who was an art historian, and he had told her some really quite interesting facts about Islamic art. Although admittedly after three hours of listening to him talking about his favourite topic her attention *had* started to wander.

'You're wrong, I'm afraid.' She was pleased that she sounded cool and collected—the opposite of how she felt. 'All I care about is doing my job to the best of my ability, and my interest in you is purely from the perspective of my role as your psychotherapist. I'm determined to discover how you tick, Jarek. You've described yourself as a prisoner,' she said gently, 'but perhaps the prison bars are inside your head.'

Jarek sprawled in the back of the limousine and considered telling the driver to turn the car around and take him back to the Frieden Clinic, so that he could jump on his motorbike and get the hell out of Dodge. But he had given his word to his brother-in-law that, for Elin's sake, he would spend six weeks undergoing psychotherapy. And, because his sister was the only person in the world whom he loved, he would stick it out even though it promised to be the most boring few weeks of his life.

Although perhaps it wouldn't be as tedious as he'd first feared, he mused, visualising the delectable Dr Maitland.

He had told her the truth—the only time he intended to do so—when he'd admitted that she was different from his expectations of her. Holly was a stunning brunette, but he had imagined her as a matronly figure, possibly wearing a tweed suit—rather like the vicar's wife in Little Bardley, who had always been kind to him when he'd been an angry teenager and constantly at loggerheads with Ralph Saunderson, his adoptive father.

But Holly looked nothing like a vicar's wife, and even her uninspiring clothes couldn't hide her gorgeous curvaceous figure. The sight of her too-tight blouse straining across her breasts, affording him a tantalising glimpse of creamy flesh where the material gaped around the buttonholes, had sent a rush of heat straight to his groin.

Frankly, she had rendered him speechless—which was not a condition Jarek often suffered from. He was clever with words, and always knew the right things to say—to women especially. That was why he could not understand why he had blurted out to Holly that she was beautiful. He'd sounded like an adolescent on a first date. Usually he was the king of cool, and the funny thing was that the more he acted as if he didn't care the more interested women were in him.

The truth was he really *didn't* care about anything or anyone apart from his sister, whom he had protected since she was a baby. But Elin was married to Cortez now, and they had a son,

Harry. Soon their second child would be born. Jarek had accepted that Elin's life had moved on and, although they would always share a close bond, that her priorities were her husband and family. Hell, he'd even accepted that Cortez, who was actually Ralph Saunderson's secret son and heir, was a decent guy.

But, while his sister deserved to be happy, Jarek knew he would never come to terms with what he had done, and the grief he had caused to both Elin and Ralph Saunderson. It was his fault that Lorna Saunderson had died, and the raw pain inside him was his punishment—it was what he deserved.

He steered his mind away from the dark path of memory, which inevitably led to the self-destructive behaviour his sister had begged him to seek help for. The truth was *no one* could help him. He pictured Dr Maitland's doe eyes and her serenely lovely face. He'd nicknamed her 'angel-face' but there was nothing angelic about her sinfully sexy mouth. He'd found himself longing to taste and explore it with his tongue.

At another time—even a month ago—he would have viewed Holly as an enjoyable distraction, and nothing would have stopped him from taking advantage of the awareness of him that she had unsuccessfully tried to hide.

But the letter he had received three weeks ago had made him question everything he'd believed he knew about himself. It had even made him wonder...who *was* Jarek Dvorska?

CHAPTER TWO

JAREK STARED OUT of the car window at the stunning Alpine landscape. All around him majestic snow-white mountains touched the sky and were reflected in a gentian-blue lake. The pine trees growing on the slopes looked as if they had been dusted with icing sugar, and here and there quaint Hansel and Gretel chalets peeped out from beneath snow-covered roofs.

The mountainous scene was exquisite, but there was also an inexplicable familiarity about it that he found puzzling. Ever since his adoptive parents had taken him on a skiing holiday in Chamonix, when he was twelve, Jarek had felt 'at home' in the mountains. But that did not make sense, because he had spent the first nine years of his life in the Bosnian capital Sarajevo. He had no recollection of his family's home in the city, but he remembered the grim grey orphanage where he and Elin had lived after their parents had died.

Why did he feel a sense of recognition when he skied down a mountain? he had once asked Lorna Saunderson, when he'd been trying to make sense of the images inside his head that he thought must be snatches of dreams—because how could they be real memories? For that matter, how had he known instinctively how to ski, without any help from an instructor, on that trip to Chamonix?

His adoptive mother—the only woman he had ever called Mama, since he had no idea who his real mother was—had reminded him that Sarajevo was surrounded by mountains. She'd suggested that perhaps staff at the orphanage had taken the children on a trip to the mountains and he had forgotten it.

Jarek thought it was unlikely. His memories of early childhood were of fear and hunger and regular beatings from the staff—although he had no idea what he might have done to merit such severe punishment. He certainly did not remember being taken out of the orphanage, and his recollections of Bosnia were only of the war that had taken place there in the nineteen-nineties, when Sarajevo had been besieged by Serbian soldiers.

His boyhood memories were of the sound of

machine gun fire and the loud explosions when bombs had fallen into the compound outside the orphanage, where the children had played. He and the other orphaned children had huddled together in a damp cellar while Sarajevo had been under fire. Sometimes the few staff who had not deserted the orphanage or been killed had been in such a rush to get down to the cellar that they'd left the babies upstairs in their cots when the bombing started.

But Jarek had always refused to abandon his little sister, and had constantly risked his life to take her down to the cellar, where she would be safe. Elin had been about a year old when the war had begun, and even then she had been remarkably pretty. When a wealthy English couple—Ralph and Lorna Saunderson—had decided to adopt a Bosnian orphan they had chosen a golden-haired angelic little girl. But Elin had become so distressed when they'd tried to separate her from her older brother that Lorna had insisted on rescuing Jarek too, and so the children had escaped hell and gone to live at stately Cuckmere Hall on the Sussex Downs.

For years Jarek had not thought too deeply

about his strange affinity with mountains. He did not take *anything* too seriously, because he was afraid that if he did the darkness in his soul might devour him. But that goddamned letter—from a man who had allegedly worked for Vostov's royal family over two decades ago—had unlocked Pandora's Box. The only way he could prevent the nightmares which had plagued him recently was to drink enough vodka so that he did not so much sleep as sink into oblivion for a few hours, if he was lucky.

He had convinced himself that the letter was a hoax and ignored it. But when he'd arrived at the Frieden Clinic and seen that newspaper headline about Vostov something had flashed into his mind that he might have believed was a deeply buried memory—if it hadn't been so crazy. Unthinkable. He didn't want to think, and he certainly wasn't going to allow Dr Holly Maitland access to the innermost secrets that his instincts warned him were best kept hidden.

'Hey, Gunther.' Jarek leaned forward to speak to the driver. 'How far is it to the chalet where I will be staying?'

'We should be there in approximately ten minutes, sir,' Gunther replied in perfect English. 'We will soon come to a town and ski resort called Arlenwald. Chalet Soline is on the other side of the town, a little higher up the mountain.'

'Does Arlenwald have any good bars?'

'Bibiana's Bar is a popular place with young people who like to drink Schnapps and watch the dancing girls. Or the Oberant Hotel is very charming. I believe they have a string quartet who play music while guests enjoy afternoon tea.'

'Hmm…tea or Schnapps—what is your preference, Gunther?'

'I am not fond of tea, sir.'

'Nor me. How about we stop at Bibiana's Bar so I can buy you a drink?'

'Dr Maitland instructed me to take you straight to the chalet,' Gunther said doubtfully.

Jarek smiled. 'There is no need to tell her that we took a short detour, is there?'

'What do you mean, he's not here?' Holly stared at Karl, the chef and butler at Chalet Soline. 'The chauffeur left the Frieden Clinic with Mr Dvorska two hours ago, to make a journey that has taken me twenty minutes.'

Admittedly the four-by-four she had used to drive herself to the chalet was better suited to the mountain roads than a limousine, but it should have taken the chauffeur no more than half an hour to deliver Jarek to the luxury alpine lodge where he would stay while he underwent a course of psychological treatment.

'I understand that Mr Dvorska wished to spend some time in Arlenwald,' Karl told her. 'Gunther telephoned to say he had left the patient in the town, because he had to attend another appointment, and that Mr Dvorska intended to walk the last part of the journey to Chalet Soline.'

Holly frowned. 'I know Gunther had to go to Salzburg today, but I expected him to follow my instructions and bring the patient here first. Goodness knows what Mr Dvorska has found to do in Arlenwald. There are only a few ski shops and hotels—and that dreadful bar where the waitresses dress up in supposedly Austrian folk costumes. I doubt the traditional dirndl was as low-cut as the dresses worn by the girls at Bibiana's Bar,' she said drily.

The lively bar, which was a popular venue for the après-ski crowd, was just the kind of place that Jarek would head for, she thought grimly. She shouldn't have let him out of her sight. Jarek's fondness for alcohol had been extensively documented in the tabloids, and she should have stuck to him like glue and escorted him to Chalet Soline herself. Instead she had sent him off with the chauffeur to give herself time to try and understand why *he*, of all men, had made her aware of her sensuality in a way she had never felt before.

Just thinking about his too-handsome face and his sexy grin that was both an invitation and a promise caused heat to unfurl in the pit of her stomach. She grimaced. Sexual alchemy was an enigma, and scientific research had yet to fully explain the complex biological and psychological reasons why one person was attracted to another. At a basic level her awareness of Jarek was the purely primal reaction of a female searching for an alpha-male, Holly reminded herself. But she was an intelligent, educated woman of the twenty-first century and she was *not* at the mercy of her hormones. She would simply have to ignore the thunder of her pulse when Jarek looked at her with that wicked glint in his eyes that made her want to respond to his unspoken challenge.

Her conscience queried whether she should ask Professor Heppel to assign a different psychotherapist to work with Jarek—except that she could not think of a good reason to request being taken off his case. She certainly could not admit that she was attracted to her patient. It would be tantamount to professional suicide.

Besides, she thought as she climbed into the four-by-four and headed towards the town that she had driven through five minutes earlier, right at this moment her feelings for Jarek Dvorska were murderous rather than amorous.

Bibiana's Bar was at the far end of Arlenwald's pretty main street. Popular with skiers and snowboarders, even at five o'clock in the afternoon the place was packed with people clutching huge steins of beer, and Holly struggled to thread her way through the crowd over to the bar. Rock music pumped out from enormous speakers and the heavy bass reverberated through her body and exacerbated her tension headache. It seemed impossible that she would be able to find Jarek in this crowd, and she didn't even know for certain that he was here.

After a fruitless search, with her head pounding in competition with the music, she was about to give up. Then her attention was drawn to two girls wearing micro mini-skirts and cropped blouses that revealed their lithe figures, who were dancing on top of a table.

Following her instincts, she made her way across the room and felt a mixture of relief and anger when she spotted Jarek sitting in an alcove. Another girl was perched on his knee, and as Holly watched him slide his hand over the girl's bare thigh her temper simmered.

Trust him to find a dark corner to commit dark deeds, she fumed. She would have loved to walk away and leave him to get on with his sordid lifestyle of booze and bimbos, but she did not relish having to confess to Professor Heppel that she had failed in her first assignment.

She became aware that Jarek was not watching the girls who were dancing so frenetically in front of him. His brilliant blue eyes were focused on her. Once again her body responded to the challenge in his bold stare and she felt her nipples pull tight. He was unfairly gorgeous, and she was helpless to prevent her body's treacherous reaction to him. The cruel beauty of his angular face and that too-long dark blond hair that he pushed off his brow with a careless flick of his hand were a killer combination. Few women would be able to resist his rampant sensuality and the devil-may-care attitude that warned he was untameable.

The girl sitting on his lap clearly found him irresistible. Holly was irritated as she watched Jarek lower his head and murmur something to the girl, who giggled as she slid off his knee and glanced over at her.

The other girls jumped down from the table and blew extravagant kisses to Jarek as they sauntered away but he ignored them, and the smouldering gaze he directed at Holly made her feel as if she was the only woman in the room. It was what he *did*, she reminded herself. He was a master of seduction. But she was not about to climb onto the table and perform a sexy dance for him. She was his therapist, for heaven's sake!

'You were expected at Chalet Soline two hours ago, but it's my fault entirely that you didn't make it,' she said breezily, to hide the fact that she wanted to strangle him. 'I should have realised I would need to babysit you to keep you out of trouble.'

His grin made her heart give an annoying flip. 'Ada, Dagna and Halfrida were no *trouble*,' he drawled. 'Especially Halfrida. She wanted to know if you are my wife, come to nag me.'

'It's a pity she didn't ask *me*. I would have told her that if I was ever interested in marrying you would be the last person I'd choose for my husband,' she said tartly, goaded by the memory of how the pretty blonde had cuddled up to him.

'Really? I'm considered quite a catch.' He sounded highly amused. 'In fact a few of the tabloids have described me as "Europe's most eligible bachelor".'

'The fact that you are a multi-millionaire no doubt goes a long way to explaining your eligibility.'

He laughed, and a gleam of admiration flickered in his eyes. 'Your name suits your prickly nature, Holly. So, would you marry for money?'

'Of course not. And as I have already said, I'm not looking for a husband.'

His brows lifted. 'I'm surprised. I had you down as the type of woman who dreams of a cottage with roses round the door, marriage to a dependable guy and a couple of babies.'

She masked the sharp stab of pain in her heart with a brisk smile. 'I grew up in the English countryside, and my experience of quaint old cottages is that they are damp and expensive to heat. I'm too busy with my career to think about marriage. Being a psychotherapist isn't a nine-to-five job—which is why I am here at...' she glanced at her watch '...ten to six in the evening to save you from yourself.'

'Maybe I don't want to be saved.' There was steel beneath his soft tone.

Holly looked pointedly at the three-quarters empty bottle of vodka on the table in front of him. 'Your notoriety with the press means you are very recognisable. For all you know, someone here in the bar might have taken a photo of you drinking and partying and posted it on social media. How do you think your sister will feel if she hears that you've wimped out of having treatment?'

His expression turned wintry. 'I have never *wimped out* of anything in my life!'

'Acknowledging and dealing with emotional baggage takes courage. It would be far easier to carry on with your selfish lifestyle, even though your drinking and wild behaviour hurts the people who love you.'

'No one loves me,' he said lightly, as if his flash of temper moments earlier hadn't happened—as if he didn't care.

Holly frowned. It was her job to understand people, but she could not read Jarek and she wasn't sure if she had heard something raw in his voice or if she had imagined it.

'Your sister must love you or she wouldn't be concerned about you,' she murmured.

His bland smile gave nothing away. 'Elin has her own family—and good luck to her. I'm glad she is happy again. I was afraid I had ruined...' He stopped speaking and his jaw clenched.

'You had ruined what?' Holly held her breath, hoping he would continue. She sensed that what he had been about to say was an important clue that might help her to fathom him out.

'It doesn't matter.'

She couldn't force him to talk to her. Patience was a therapist's most valuable tool, she reminded herself. And nor could she drag him out of the bar. So she stood there, wondering with a growing sense of panic what her plan of action would be if he refused to leave.

To her relief he stood up and raised his arms above his head, giving an indolent stretch that caused the bottom of his sweater to rise up a little and reveal golden skin above the waistband of his trousers.

Her eyes were drawn to that strip of bare torso, covered with a fuzz of dark blond hair that disappeared beneath his trousers, and heat swept through her as her wayward imagination pictured where the hairs grew more thickly...around the base of his manhood.

His voice jolted her from her thoughts, and she flushed, praying he had not guessed her wanton imaginings.

'While I am touched by your desire to save me,' he drawled, 'I can't help wondering if your concern is more about proving to Professor Heppel that he was justified in offering you a job at his clinic. Gunther mentioned that you were only recently appointed at the Frieden Clinic.'

'Believe it or not, I care about doing a good job and I genuinely want to help you.' She tried to ignore her guilt that there was an element of truth in his words.

To her relief he said no more as he picked up his jacket and followed her out of the bar. A tense silence filled the four-by-four while she drove them to Chalet Soline, and she could think of nothing to say to lighten his mood—which had become grimmer still when they arrived at the alpine lodge and were greeted by Karl.

The chef-butler ushered them into the wood-panelled sitting room, where a fire was blazing in the hearth and deep leather sofas piled with colourful cushions created a sense of stylish informality. Jarek gave a cursory glance at his surroundings as he crossed to one of the tall windows and stared out at the dark winter's night.

'It goes without saying that I will hold everything you choose to tell me during our sessions in absolute confidence,' Holly said quietly as she watched him prowl around the room.

He was like a caged wolf, simmering with silent fury. She was surprised he wasn't showing any obvious signs of being drunk, even though he had consumed enough vodka to render him unconscious. Thankfully he hadn't staggered out of Bibiana's Bar—or, worse, needed to be carried out to the car by burly security staff. She did not want Professor Heppel to find out that her client had been caught drinking in a bar within an hour of checking into the Frieden Clinic.

'I hope you will be comfortable at Chalet Soline. Karl is an excellent chef, and the maid, Beatrice, will take care of the house. I'll show you up to the master suite. You'll probably want to take some time to settle in and freshen up before you meet Professor Heppel this evening.'

She dared not suggest that he might need to sober up, but the hard gleam in his eyes told her he had understood perfectly well what she'd meant.

'I don't need a nursemaid or a babysitter.'

He crossed the room in long strides and halted in front of her, so close that she breathed in the spicy scent of his aftershave and her senses went haywire.

'And I definitely do not need a prissy, much too pretty psychologist to patronise me.'

Holly was disgusted with herself for the way her heart leapt at his offhand compliment. Flirting was second nature to him, she reminded herself. He hadn't singled her out specially, and she would *not* respond to the blazing heat in his eyes.

'I know what *you* need,' he drawled, his voice lowering so that it became wickedly suggestive and sent a shiver of reaction down her spine.

She arched her brows. 'Enlighten me.'

He gave a wolfish smile. 'You need to buy a bigger blouse.'

Holly followed his gaze down her body and was mortified to see that a button on her blouse had popped open and her lacy bra was showing. Blushing hotly, she attempted to refasten the blouse, but Jarek moved faster and his knuckles brushed the upper slopes of her breasts as he slid the button into the buttonhole.

The brief touch of his skin on hers made her tremble. Goosebumps rose on her flesh and her nipples jerked to attention. The mocking gleam in Jarek's eyes dared her to make the excuse again that she was cold, now they were inside the warm chalet.

She was tempted to wipe the smug smile off his face with the sharp impact of her palm against his jaw, but managed to restrain herself from behaving so unprofessionally.

He swung away from her and raked a hand though his hair, almost as if he had been as shocked by the bolt of electricity that had shot between them as she had.

His manner changed and he said abruptly, 'Is there a room that I can use for an office? I want to get on with some work.'

'There's a small study along the hall. But you are supposed to be using your stay at the Frieden Clinic as a retreat from the stresses of your everyday life—and that includes taking a break from work so that you can focus on exploring your emotions.'

Jarek gave her a sardonic look. 'My company, Dvorska Holdings, employs several hundred people. I am also the executive director of a charity, and take an active role in the day-to-day running of the organisation. I can't abandon my responsibilities to my staff—or to the great number of volunteers who give up their time to support Lorna's Gift.'

He laughed softly.

'As for exploring my emotions... 'I'll quote a famous female American journalist and advice columnist called Dorothy Dix, who said, *"Confession is always weakness. The grave soul keeps its own secrets, and takes its own punishment in silence."'*

What had he meant by that? Holly wondered as she watched Jarek stride out of the room. She couldn't keep pace with his mercurial changes of mood. Just when she had been convinced that he was the disreputable playboy portrayed by the tabloids, and a shameless flirt with a ready line of sexual innuendo, he had surprised her by sounding as if he genuinely cared about his role with a charity.

She knew that he was co-director with his sister of Lorna's Gift—a charitable organisation that raised money to support children living in orphanages around the world. But she had assumed that Jarek was simply a figurehead for the charity, and it was disconcerting to discover that he took some things seriously.

It would be easier if he *was* nothing more than fodder for the celebrity-obsessed paparazzi, she thought, because then she could dismiss her reaction to his potent sensuality as a temporary aberration.

Holly rubbed her hand across her brow to try to ease her tension headache and glanced at the clock. Professor Heppel was due to arrive for dinner at Chalet Soline in two hours, which gave her time for a soak in the hot tub and a chance to get a grip on her wayward emotions.

The next time she met Jarek she was determined to be coolly professional.

Jarek switched off his laptop, having finalised another successful business deal. The one thing he could rely on in the grim mess that was his life was his ability to make money, he thought cynically. Although he had not always been lucky.

Over the past two years his instinct for correctly guessing how global markets would perform had catapulted him onto the list of the world's top ten most successful traders, and enabled him to recoup the huge losses he'd made at Saunderson's Bank.

That embarrassing episode had resulted from an unfortunate combination of events. He had taken a particularly risky gamble on the Asian stockmarkets, and an earthquake in Japan had led to a temporary suspension of trading on the Nikkei—with disastrous consequences for his investments and the near-collapse of one of England's oldest and most prestigious private banks.

Ralph Saunderson had probably turned in his grave, Jarek thought sardonically. He had been a feral boy of nearly ten when he had been taken from war-ravaged Sarajevo to live at Cuckmere Hall, and his resistance to authority had meant that there had been no love lost between him and Ralph. Following his adoptive father's death, he had been shocked to discover that he had been excluded from Ralph's will, and that Cortez Ramos—Ralph's biological son—had inherited Cuckmere Hall and the chairmanship of Saunderson's Bank.

He knew why Ralph had chosen Cortez to be his heir. Ralph had blamed him, Jarek, for Lorna Saunderson's death, and Jarek had for once agreed with his adoptive father.

He was haunted by memories of when his adoptive mother had been fatally shot by an armed raider during a robbery at a jeweller's. The four years that had passed since that terrible day had not dimmed the images in his mind of Lorna lying crumpled on the floor, and Elin kneeling beside her sobbing hysterically. The keening cry his sister had given when she'd realised that her adored mama was dead would echo in his head for ever.

In Sarajevo, Jarek had seen the bodies of dead soldiers and heard the rattling last breaths of young men—some of whom had been teenagers, only a few years older than him. He'd thought that nothing could be worse than the atrocities he'd seen in that bloody and brutal civil war, but the knowledge that Mama had died because of *his* reckless attempt to overpower the gunman was an agony that would be with him for ever.

He would never forgive himself, even though Elin loyally insisted that he wasn't to blame.

It had been his idea to set up a charity to support orphans in honour of Lorna Saunderson and, ironically, his willingness to take risks on the stockmarket meant he had earned a fortune for Lorna's Gift. It was some kind of reparation for what he had done, but nothing would ever ease his guilt.

God knew what a psychologist would make of him if he ever revealed the dark torment in his soul, Jarek thought grimly. But he had no intention of *exploring his emotions* with the deliciously sexy Dr Maitland.

Some things were best left alone—which was why he had decided not to respond to the request he had received from the head of the National Council of Vostov, asking him to have a DNA test which might prove that he was related to Vostov's royal family, who had all perished in a car accident twenty years ago.

There was no possibility that it could be true, he assured himself. The idea was ridiculous. But what if his nightmares were *not* simply horrific figments of his imagination? his conscience whispered. It would mean that the images in his mind were of real events, real people...*his parents*.

At the orphanage he had been told that his mother and father had been killed early in the war, when the apartment block where they'd lived had been destroyed by a bomb. Jarek and his baby sister had been pulled from the rubble and the trauma had wiped out all his memories of his life before that day.

He'd accepted the explanation eventually— after he had been beaten by the orphanage staff whenever he'd talked about his strange dreams. But now his nightmares had returned, more vivid and terrible than when he was a boy. And if the scenes that played out in his subconscious mind *were* real events then he had something even more devastating than his adoptive mother's death on his conscience.

Jarek pushed his hair off his brow and acknowledged that if he had not been stuck halfway up a mountain he would have headed to the nearest bar and sought to escape the demons inside him with another bottle of vodka and an attractive blonde—or two. He remembered the girls at Bibiana's Bar and for a moment was tempted to take the four-by-four parked outside the chalet and drive himself to Arlenwald, to hook up with Halfrida and her friends.

It would be worth it just to ruffle Dr Maitland's feathers.

His lips twitched as he remembered Holly's

outraged expression when she'd discovered him in the bar. The truth was he would like to do more than *ruffle* her, he brooded. His body stirred as he pictured her delectable curves. She was an intriguing mix of uptight schoolmistress and sensual siren, and Jarek couldn't remember the last time he had been intrigued by a woman.

If she had been someone other than his psychologist… Hell, if *he* had been someone else— someone better than the man he knew he was—he would have enjoyed allowing their mutual sexual attraction to reach its logical conclusion and taken her to bed.

But Holly had stated that she wanted to find out what made him tick, and he was utterly determined to prevent her from uncovering the secrets buried deep in his soul.

CHAPTER THREE

JAREK FOUND AN outlet for his restless energy in the chalet's gym. He could think of other, more enjoyable ways to get hot and sweaty than pounding his fists into a punch-bag. But he had promised his brother-in-law there would be no more scandalous stories about his personal life in the tabloids—which meant that until Elin's baby was born he had to keep away from bars and airhead blondes who were attracted to his multi-millionaire status and bad-boy image.

The truth was he'd never cared about what was printed about him—which was mostly lies. Any publicity, good or bad, was publicity for Lorna's Gift, and he seized every opportunity to promote the vital work of the charity.

But Elin's husband Cortez took a different view.

'Elin gets upset when she sees your name in newspaper headlines or on the pages of gossip magazines, invariably with intimate details of your sex-life,' Cortez had warned him. 'She has gestational high blood pressure, which could lead to more serious complications with her pregnancy, and her obstetrician says it is crucial she doesn't suffer any stress that could cause her blood pressure to rise even higher.'

Jarek shared his brother-in-law's concern. Elin and Cortez had not been together when Elin had nearly died giving birth to their first child, and it had been Jarek who had sat by her bed in ITU, willing her to pull through for the sake of her baby son in the hospital nursery.

There were worse places to spend the next few weeks than the spectacular Austrian Alps, he mused. Chalet Soline offered six-star luxury, and next to the well-equipped gym there was a sauna room while outside on the decked area stood a hot tub. He *would* find it relaxing after his punishing workout to lie in a bubbling hot tub and look up at the snow-covered mountains, or count the stars that glittered diamond-bright in the night sky.

But when he glanced at his watch he realised he did not have time before Professor Heppel arrived.

About to head back to his room, to shower before dinner, he glanced out of a window and noticed that the lights had been switched on around the hot tub. Steam was curling up from the surface of the water, forming wispy white clouds against the black night sky.

Jarek stopped dead and stared at the figure of a woman rising out of the steam like a mystical goddess. And what a figure! He swallowed as he watched Holly wade across to the edge of the pool. It was no exaggeration to say that she was a goddess, with an hourglass figure that was reminiscent of the silver screen sirens from a previous era, like Sophia Loren and Elizabeth Taylor.

She was wearing a one-piece swimsuit with cut-out sections at the sides that drew attention to her slender waist. Jarek wanted to explore the tantalising areas of her bare skin on display with his hands. He lifted his eyes higher to her voluptuous breasts, barely contained within the tiny triangles of gold material that formed the bra cups of the swimsuit, and felt himself harden. He was fascinated by her daring choice of swimwear, which was such a contrast to the unexciting clothes she'd worn earlier.

Moving his gaze lower, he followed the rounded curves of her hips and her toned thighs, exposed by the swimsuit's high-cut legs.

Who was the real Holly? he wondered. The serious psychologist, or the sizzling sex bomb who made the blood thunder in his veins? His body felt taut and energised after his gym workout and he wanted—quite possibly more than he'd ever wanted anything in his life, he discovered— to pull Holly beneath him and ease her stretchy swimsuit aside so that he could thrust his rock-solid erection home.

It was lucky he had worn loose sweatpants for his session in the gym, Jarek thought derisively. He was so turned on by the sight of Holly in her barely there swimsuit that he felt he might explode.

His common sense told him to head back to his room. But he rarely heeded good advice.

The temperature outside the chalet was way below zero, and as the icy air hit his heated skin every nerve-ending in his body tingled.

Jarek allowed the door to thud closed behind him as he stepped outside onto the wooden decking. The sound caused Holly to jerk her head round, and she gave a startled cry when she saw him, followed by a curse when she dropped the towel that she had just picked up from the deck into the water.

'You startled me. I thought you were working in the study,' she muttered in an embarrassed voice, as if he had caught her naked—which she very nearly was, Jarek mused as he roamed his eyes over her insubstantial swimsuit and felt the ache in his groin clamour to be appeased.

He did not reply, for the simple reason that he could not think of anything to say—couldn't think of anything at all but how utterly perfect she was with her skin flushed pink from the heat of the hot tub and a deeper flush on her pretty face.

Her hair was piled on top of her head and loose tendrils curled about her cheeks. She was a luscious goddess, and he wanted nothing more than to drop to his knees in front of her to worship her bounteous beauty with his mouth and explore every secret place on her body with his tongue.

He was jolted from his sexual haze by the sound of her clipped voice.

'Would you please pass me another towel?

There's a pile of clean towels on the shelf outside the sauna room,' she said when he didn't move, just stared at her while he tried to control the conflagration of lust that burned down to his bones.

'Jarek, for heaven's sake—I'm freezing.'

He couldn't tear his gaze from the prominent points of her nipples, clearly outlined beneath her clingy swimsuit. His mouth went dry as he imagined peeling the swimsuit from her breasts to feast his eyes and then his lips on those provocative peaks.

Somehow he forced himself to turn and walk into the house, and he grabbed a towel before retracing his steps back across the decking.

Holly held out her hand for the towel, but Jarek did not pass it to her immediately. 'First let your hair down,' he growled.

'Are you kidding?' Her brown eyes widened. There was shock, anger and something else that was harder to define but made him ache even more, in her expression.

'Do you want me to catch pneumonia?'

She didn't wait for him to reply—which was probably a good thing, he acknowledged, because he would have to admit that what he *wanted* was her legs wrapped around his back.

Throwing him a look of sheer irritation, she lifted her hands up and released the clip on top of her head so that her hair tumbled down around her shoulders in glossy waves of rich chocolate-brown. 'Satisfied?'

He doubted he would ever be satisfied again with the too thin, too blonde, brittle women who came and went from his bed in an endless stream of unmemorable sexual encounters. They *always* came, he thought sardonically. He was as good at sex as he was at making money, yet neither activity ever filled the emptiness inside him.

Finally he heeded his common sense, aware that indulging his sexual desire for Holly might satisfy him temporarily but that he would soon grow bored of her. It was just how he was: 'a restless soul', Mama had once described him, while his adoptive father had accused him of being reckless. Ralph had been proved right.

He gave Holly the towel and she immediately dragged it around her shoulders to hide her gorgeous body from him before she stepped out of the hot tub and stalked back to the chalet.

Jarek caught up with her in a few long strides. 'Why are you here?' he demanded, placing his hand on her arm to prevent her walking through the door that led from the gym annexe into the main part of the house.

'Where else would I be?' She tensed beneath his hand and with obvious reluctance raised her eyes to his face.

'I assumed you had gone to wherever you live. Do you rent a place in Salzburg? Or is there staff accommodation at the Frieden Clinic, where we met earlier?'

She frowned. 'I live here—at Chalet Soline. When I'm in London I share a flat with a friend, but for my job with the Frieden Clinic I am required to live at one of the clinic's residences so that I can provide psychological support around the clock. Every member of the clinical team is assigned to a chalet, where they treat patients on an individual basis. Professor Heppel came up with the radical approach of providing access to twenty-four-seven treatment, rather than sessions which last for an hour once or twice a week. His highly successful method is explained in the brochure that you didn't bother to read—

and I also explained the set-up when I met you at the clinic's reception centre earlier today. But you seemed more interested in reading a story in the newspaper than listening to me.'

Holly's disapproving tone reminded Jarek of the headmistress who had expelled him from his exclusive private school at the age of fifteen, after he had been caught smuggling alcohol into the school and selling it to the other boys. He had argued that his business venture had shown entrepreneurial spirit, but the headmistress had warned that his rebellious nature would ultimately be his ruin.

He thought of the newspaper headline that had seized his attention when he had arrived at the Frieden Clinic.

What did happen to Vostov's royal children?

Jarek feared the answer was buried in his subconscious mind, and that his nightmares might reveal a truth that was too shocking for him to contemplate. Certainly he could not risk Holly hearing him shout out in his sleep, as had happened on one of the rare occasions when he had spent a whole night with a woman he had picked up in a bar.

The next morning Tara… Tyra—he hadn't taken much heed of her name—had said he'd kept her awake with his shouting and maybe he should talk to a psychiatrist or something about the crazy stuff in his head.

Jarek's chosen method of preventing his bad dreams was to drink enough vodka until he was unconscious. But without access to alcohol God knew what his nightmares might reveal.

He realised that Holly was speaking again. 'I believe you will find it beneficial to be able to discuss issues with your therapist whenever you need to, instead of having to wait for an allotted time for treatment sessions. If you want to talk to me in the middle of the night you can ring through to my room and wake me up. Part of my job is to be available whenever you want me.'

'Is that so…?'

Jarek felt the hard thud of his pulse and knew he had to resist it—had to resist *her*. There was a curious innocence about Holly that made him want to protect her from himself.

'There is only *one* reason why I would wake

you in the middle of the night, angel-face,' he drawled, 'and it wouldn't be because I want to talk.'

He watched a scarlet stain spread over her face and wondered when he had last seen a woman blush. For a few seconds he felt a tug of regret, because he could not allow this shimmering, ephemeral thing between them that was something other than sexual attraction—something *more*—to flourish. He was who he was: reckless, rebellious, with a knack of destroying everything that was good in his life.

'There you go again with the sexual innuendo.' She put her head on one side and studied him intently. 'Are you trying to frighten me? Because I have to tell you that you aren't succeeding.'

'You *should* be afraid of me,' he said roughly. 'I am everything you have read about me and worse.' He wanted to shout at her that he didn't deserve the sympathy he could see in her velvet brown eyes. His jaw clenched. 'This is a complication I don't need right now.'

She wrinkled her nose and Jarek swore silently. He didn't *do* cute, his brain insisted, but his body paid no attention.

'What do you mean by "this"? she asked, looking puzzled.

He stretched out his hand and jerked the edges of the towel she was clutching around her from her fingers. With a cry of protest she tried to snatch it back, but he whipped it away from her body and trailed his eyes with slow deliberation over her skimpy swimsuit. Desire kicked hard in his gut as he stared at her lush breasts, half-spilling over the top of the swimsuit, and the hard points of her nipples that betrayed her so sweetly.

'This,' he growled, moving his hand over her body from her throat to her hips, but not actually touching her. Not quite.

He heard her catch her breath and it took all his will power to resist stroking his fingertips across her skin.

'You can deny the sexual attraction between us all you like,' he taunted, 'but your body is sending out a different message.'

He dropped his gaze to where the sides of her swimsuit were cut away and decided he would happily give away his entire fortune if he could trace his hands over the tantalising areas of bare skin. But if he touched her he did not trust himself to be able to stop. He couldn't remember ever feeling so hungry for a woman, but no doubt the restless ache inside him was because he hadn't had sex for almost a month.

He wanted Holly so badly simply because she was there in front of him, wearing a sexy swimsuit, and because he'd never had to deny himself a woman before.

It was an inconvenient time to discover that he had scruples, he thought sardonically. Delectable Dr Maitland was off-limits, and he had to content himself with stepping closer to her.

He noticed the pulse at the base of her throat beating erratically. 'Believe me, I'm tempted to accept the invitation you are sending out, angel-face,' he told her softly. 'But it will cause a lot less trouble for both of us if I cancel my booking with the clinic before we do something that *you* might regret and *I* will forget far too easily.'

Anger flashed in her eyes. 'Any invitation is purely in your imagination,' she said tightly. And then a note of panic edged into her voice. 'You *can't* be thinking of leaving the Frieden Clinic? You told me that you had assured your brother-in-law you would undergo psychotherapy to deal with your anger issues and allay your sister's concerns about you.'

He shrugged. 'I told Cortez I would keep off the paparazzi's radar until Elin has the baby. As long as I keep out of trouble there is no reason for my sister to find out that I decided not to remain at the clinic.'

'She will find out when she asks me for an update on how you are responding to treatment.'

Jarek stiffened. 'Are you intending to make weekly reports on my progress? Perhaps I'll earn a gold star if I'm a good boy,' he said with icy sarcasm. He shook his head. 'I can't *believe* my sister asked you to *spy* on me. Or that you agreed. What happened to your promise to respect my confidentiality?'

'Not spy on you,' she denied quickly. 'Elin phoned me before you arrived, and it's obvious that she cares about you and is concerned about your emotional health.' Holly's voice faltered when he swore. 'Your sister asked me to call her if you refused to stay. I won't lie to her and pretend you are receiving treatment.'

'So the Frieden Clinic *is* my prison and *you* are my gaoler—albeit a very beautiful one,' Jarek drawled, in the lazy tone he had perfected over many years in order to hide his true thoughts.

He acknowledged that he could not leave the clinic and risk upsetting Elin, but that meant he was trapped at Chalet Soline with Holly.

There might be *some* benefits to his enforced captivity, he mused. The Frieden Clinic prided itself on its exclusivity, and guarded the privacy and anonymity of its wealthy clientele. Nobody, apart from Elin and Cortez, knew of his whereabouts, and he hoped 'the Vostov problem' would disappear when the principality's National Council could not find him to repeat their request for him to have a DNA test.

He was no *prince*, he brooded. He was plain Jarek Dvorska. And his parents—if only he could remember them, God rest their souls—had been poor peasants. That was what the staff at the orphanage had told him. His parents had definitely *not* been Prince Goran and his consort Princess Isidora who, with their young son and baby daughter, had died in a car accident on a mountain pass as the family had attempted to escape from Vostov into neighbouring Croatia during the Balkan conflict.

Jarek pulled his thoughts back to the present. He guessed Holly was looking tense because she was worried that her first patient at the Frieden Clinic was about to walk out and that would *not* be a good start in her new job.

He let his eyes roam over her, noting the rich coffee and chocolate tones of her silky hair and those huge Bambi eyes fringed by impossibly long lashes. Her sensual mouth would tempt a saint, let alone the sinner he knew he was.

He shrugged. For once in his life he had tried to do the right thing, but fate had decided to throw him and Holly together and he wasn't about to complain. She would be an entertaining distraction. He had promised Cortez he would keep his private life out of the media's spotlight, but he hadn't taken a vow of celibacy.

He let go of Holly's arm and she immediately bolted away, without pausing to cover herself with the towel. Jarek felt anticipation jolt through him, hot and fierce, as he watched her race down the hallway. His eyes were drawn to the delightful curves of her derriere that were barely covered by her tiny swimsuit.

The next few weeks promised to be interesting.

CHAPTER FOUR

THE MINUTE HOLLY reached her bedroom she pulled off her swimsuit and kicked it across the floor in an uncharacteristic display of temper. But *really*! Jarek's arrogant belief that he was God's gift to womankind was *infuriating*.

She was annoyed with herself for the way she had responded to him. Her swimsuit revealed a lot more of her body than she was comfortable with, and it must have given the wrong impression about her. She'd looked more like a porn star rather than a doctor of psychology, she thought, hot with embarrassment. If she had been wearing her functional navy blue one-piece it was doubtful that Jarek would have given her a second look, let alone stared at her with the undisguised hunger in his eyes that had evoked a shocking throb of need low in her pelvis.

She blamed Kate, her flatmate in London. Holly hadn't packed any swimwear when she'd come to Austria to work at the Frieden Clinic, but then Professor Heppel had told her she could use the sauna and hot tub at Chalet Soline, and she had asked Kate to post her swimsuit to her. Unfortunately her friend had sent the frivolous gold swimsuit that she'd bought on an impulse for that disastrous—as it had turned out—holiday to Barbados with Stuart.

A glance at the clock warned Holly that there was only twenty minutes before the clinic's medical director was due to arrive at the chalet for dinner. After bundling her hair into a waterproof cap she hurried into the shower, and while she stood beneath the spray her mind flew back to the time when she had told Stuart that she was unable to have children.

It was not a conversation she had expected to have with him, when they had only been dating for eight months. But Stuart had surprised her on the second evening of their holiday by talking about the future.

'My father is considering making me a partner in the family law firm and he has made it clear that he would like me to settle down. I feel that it's time for me to think about getting married and raising a family of my own.'

They had been strolling along the beach when he had stopped and taken hold of Holly's hand.

'I would like you to be my wife, Holly. We share the same values and we both have successful careers. I can't think of anyone else I'd rather have as the mother of my children.'

Stuart had not sworn undying love for her, but that hadn't made it any easier for Holly to tell him she could not give him a child because she had a rare syndrome which meant she had been born without a womb.

Finding out when she was fifteen that she had Mayer Rokitansky Kuster Hauser syndrome— commonly shortened to MRKH—had been devastating, but at the time of her diagnosis her infertility had not been as much of an issue as her feeling that she was not 'normal'.

The syndrome meant that she had been born with a shortened vagina, and she would need surgery to enable her to have sex. As a teenager she had found it excruciatingly embarrassing to discuss intimate details about her body with her doctors, and it had been frankly impossible to talk about her condition with her parents. She had felt too self-conscious to go on dates until she was at university, and her few sexual experiences had been uncomfortable—probably because she had been so tense, she acknowledged.

Deciding when to bring up the subject of her condition and her infertility with men she dated had always been difficult. If she mentioned it on a first date it seemed pushy, and gave the impression that she was hoping for a physical long-term relationship. But if she waited weeks or months it seemed dishonest.

'I wish you had told me earlier in our relationship,' had been Stuart's response after she had broken the news that she was infertile. 'Having a child is important to me.'

Holly had refrained from pointing out that something like one in seven couples experienced problems conceiving, and that having children was not an automatic right. But Stuart's reaction had re-awoken the feeling of inadequacy that she had struggled with since she had been diagnosed with MRKH syndrome. It was true she hadn't been madly in love with Stuart, but his rejection had still hurt—especially when she'd heard a few months after they had broken up that his new girlfriend was pregnant.

She dragged her mind back to the present and stepped out of the shower to dry herself before hurrying into the bedroom to get dressed. Her dusky-pink cashmere dress had been an extravagant purchase, but its simple elegance was worth the price tag. She accessorised it with a wide belt and matching grey kitten-heel shoes.

It was an outfit she had worn several times before, and always felt comfortable in, but tonight when she looked in the mirror she decided that the dress moulded her curvaceous figure a little too lovingly. But it was five minutes to eight, and she only had time to pull a comb through her hair before she hurried downstairs.

She found Karl in the dining room, rearranging the table settings. 'Professor Heppel telephoned a few minutes ago and apologised. He cannot come for dinner this evening because his mother is unwell and he must go to Vienna to visit her,' the chef told her. 'The professor also asked me to tell you that he has booked tickets for you and Mr Dvorska to attend the masquerade ball which will take place in Salzburg next weekend.'

Holly's heart sank at the prospect of having dinner alone with Jarek while her mind still insisted on replaying those moments by the hot tub, when sexual chemistry had sizzled between them.

She watched Karl light the candles in the centre of the table. A fire was crackling in the hearth and the lamps had been turned down low, creating a dangerously intimate feel to the dining room. 'Perhaps Mr Dvorska would prefer to have his dinner served in the lounge in front of the television,' she murmured. 'I'm happy to eat in the kitchen.'

'It's bad for the digestion to eat at the same time as doing another activity.'

The lazy drawl sounded from behind her and Holly's stomach tied itself into a knot as she swung round and saw Jarek stroll through the door.

Undoubtedly *he* would unsettle her digestive system, she thought. Butterflies had leapt in her stomach when he had appeared by the hot tub, wearing a pair of sweatpants that sat low on his hips and a black gym vest that had revealed too much of his sleek, golden-skinned body. Her blood had run hot in her veins when he'd stared at her with a hard glitter in his eyes that had made her wish she could respond to his unspoken challenge.

At least now they were both dressed—but Jarek looked no less devastating in close-fitting black trousers and a black silk shirt unbuttoned at the throat to reveal a sprinkling of dark blond chest hair. Holly shivered, despite the heat from the roaring fire. There was something elemental and sensual about a real fire, and her wayward imagination pictured her and Jarek lying on the fur rug in front of the hearth, their naked limbs entwined.

She did not dare look at him for fear that he would somehow guess her thoughts. What was *wrong* with her? she asked herself in silent despair. The truth was that Jarek's rampant sex appeal made her aware of her sensuality in a way she had never felt before.

'Dr Maitland and I will have dinner in here,' Jarek said to Karl.

He pulled out a chair for Holly, leaving her no option but to sit down at the table, and as she inhaled the spicy scent of his aftershave something visceral tugged in the pit of her stomach.

'Don't look so tense.' He sounded amused. 'I don't bite.'

His wide grin revealed his white teeth and once again he reminded Holly of a wolf.

'Unless you would *like* me to bite you,' he said softly. 'Pleasure can be enhanced by a little pain, don't you find?'

She swallowed and forced herself to look at him calmly across the table, where he had taken his place opposite her. 'You have to stop this. I'm sure you automatically flirt with every woman you meet, but I suspect that your sexually suggestive remarks are designed to distract me from doing my job.'

Fortunately Karl reappeared then, to serve the first course. Holly picked up her glass and took a sip of elderflower water, wishing she could have a glass of wine—or preferably a *vat* of wine, she thought ruefully. She needed something to render her unconscious, so she did not have to cope with Jarek's teasing remarks that made her feel crazily out of control and in danger of doing something very stupid…like walk around the table and kiss his too sexy mouth to shut him up.

She stared down at her bowl of potato soup with little dumplings. It was an Austrian speciality and one of her favourites, but she found that her appetite had disappeared.

It was her professional duty to help Jarek feel at ease, she reminded herself. Patients were often reluctant to talk about their problems and she was trained to break down barriers gently.

Once Karl had left the room she murmured, 'I have read through your notes, but it would help me to gain a better understanding of you if you could tell me about the issues that led to your decision to seek psychotherapy.'

'I agreed to try therapy because other people believe I have issues,' he said sardonically. 'And before I allow you to dig around in my emotions, it only seems fair for you to tell me about yourself. You *did* say it is important for therapist and patient to establish a bond of trust,' he reminded her.

'That's true,' Holly acknowledged. 'But I assumed that Professor Heppel had showed you my

CV, which gives details of all my professional qualifications.'

'I meant that I want to get to know you on a *personal* level.'

He trapped her gaze with his, and even though the table was between them it wasn't nearly wide enough for Holly's liking. She had a sense that his piercing blue eyes could see inside her head and that he *knew* she was helpless to control the way he affected her.

It struck her then that Jarek had no intention of revealing his thoughts—or, as he put it, allowing her *to dig around in his emotions*. His scathing opinion of psychotherapy would make her job even harder.

'Who *is* Holly Maitland?' he said softly, as if he was genuinely interested and his question *wasn't* simply another diversionary tactic.

She shrugged. 'What do you want to know?'

'You mentioned that you lived in the country-side. Where *was* that, exactly?'

'I grew up on my parents' farm in Cumbria. It's a beautiful part of the world, but the farm is in a remote area of the fells, seven miles from the nearest village. It sounds romantic to live on a desolate, windswept moor,' she said with a faint smile, 'but when I was a child I felt very isolated.'

'Do you have brothers and sisters?'

'A brother—Callum. He's five years older than me, and when we were children he was always helping my father. Cal will inherit the farm one day, and now that he and his wife have a little boy it means that Maitland Farm will remain in the family, as it has done for five generations.'

Holly hoped Jarek had not noticed the slight tremor in her voice when she had mentioned her nephew. Daniel was six months old, and when she'd held him soon after he was born she had felt sad, knowing she would never hold her own baby. But just as bad had been her guilt that she was a disappointment to her mother.

She supposed it was natural that her mum had grown close to Callum's wife. After all, Brenna had given Ann Maitland a longed-for grandchild, which was something her daughter could never do. It was immature to feel envious of the bond between her mother and sister-in-law, Holly reminded herself.

'So why did a farmer's daughter decide to become a psychologist?' Jarek asked.

'I didn't know I wanted to study psychology when I left school.' She sighed. 'To be honest, all I wanted was to live somewhere with a population greater than fifty. When I was offered a place at a university in London to study modern languages I couldn't wait to experience city life.'

'Did your parents understand why you wanted to leave the farm?'

Holly felt a familiar stab of guilt. It was not an exaggeration to say that her moving away from home had felt like a betrayal of her family's long history of farming the desolate Cumbrian fells. She glanced at Jarek, surprised that a man who actively encouraged the press's portrayal of him as shallow and only interested in the pursuit of pleasure had asked such an unexpectedly intuitive question.

'I'm not sure that either of my parents have ever understood me,' she admitted. 'The farm is their life, but even as a child I knew I wanted to do something else. Mum wanted to pass on to me the traditions she had learned from her mother and grandmother, and she was disappointed that I had no interest in learning how to make jam or spin wool. I've always felt that I fall short of being the kind of daughter my mother hoped for...especially when I found out that I—'

Holly broke off abruptly, shocked that she had opened up so much to Jarek. There was no reason to tell him that she had a rare syndrome which meant she was infertile.

'That you...what?' he prompted.

A look of impatience flashed on his face when the door opened to admit Karl bringing the main course, but Holly was grateful for the interruption.

'What were you about to say?' Jarek asked, as soon the chef had finished serving the meal and departed from the room.

'Oh...' She pretended to look vague. 'I don't remember.'

His eyes narrowed on her flushed face, but to her relief he did not pursue the subject. 'What did you think of city life when you moved to London?'

'Truthfully, I found it a little overwhelming. But I was spotted by a model agency scout in my first term at university and thought I could do a bit of modelling to earn some money. Quite unexpectedly I became a successful photographic model. It seemed glamorous at first, but trying to juggle my studies with photo shoots and the frenetic social life that was part of the modelling scene affected my health—both physically and emotionally.'

Holly put down her knife and fork, unable to eat any more of the rich pork dish.

'On the surface I appeared to have a fantastic life,' she told Jarek, 'but I put on an act to hide the fact that I was finding the pressure hard to deal with. Luckily the university arranged for me to see a wonderful counsellor, who helped me through that difficult period in my life. Having personal experience of the benefits of counselling was the reason I switched to a combined psychology and psychotherapy degree.'

Counselling had helped her to accept that she had been born with MRKH syndrome, Holly thought to herself. With her counsellor's support she had worked through her grief that she was infertile, and she had even stopped believing—mostly—that she was a disappointment to her parents. But she had not completely overcome the body image issues that had worsened when she'd started modelling.

Men had desired her for the way she looked, but she had felt a fraud because, in her mind, she wasn't a *normal* woman. She had been ashamed of her body, and counselling had not completely banished her insecurities. What man would want to make love to a woman who had to use dilators before she could have sex?

She glanced at Jarek, the infamous playboy whose list of lovers was reputedly longer than a telephone directory, and a cold dose of reality washed over her. He was flirting with her because he couldn't help himself, but she was sure the smouldering desire in his eyes would quickly disappear if he discovered that he would need patience to arouse her fully before he could make love to her.

She remembered reading a tabloid story in which a well-known stage actress had claimed she'd had sex with Jarek in her dressing room during the ten-minute interval of a West End play. Maybe there was an added thrill to spontaneous sex, Holly brooded, but for her a quickie was out of the question.

She bit her lip. Why was she imagining having sex with Jarek? There was no chance of it happening. Firstly because it would be ethically and morally wrong for her to have an affair with a client, and secondly because the pretty girls at Bibiana's Bar were more his type than an unexciting psychologist who had a hang-up about sex.

Knowing those things made it easier to resist his sexy charm when he suggested they sit by the fire to drink their coffee. She gave him a cool smile and felt a spurt of satisfaction when he looked surprised. No doubt he was used to women falling at his feet, but *she* was immune to his potency she told herself firmly.

Jarek lowered his long frame onto the sofa in front of the fire and patted the empty place next to him. But Holly walked straight past and sat down in the armchair furthest away.

His phone rang and his hard features softened when he looked at the screen. 'Do you mind if I answer this?'

'Be my guest,' she murmured.

She guessed the caller was a woman when he stood up and strolled over to the window, speaking into the phone in a low tone. Once or twice he laughed softly, and Holly felt an inexplicable ache beneath her breastbone. She wasn't lonely, she assured herself. She had plenty of friends.

But recently several of her close friends had got married, and at dinner parties the conversation tended to be about pregnancy and childcare. It would be nice to have someone special to share laughs with, to share her life with, she acknowledged, but she hadn't dated anyone since Stuart.

She had a good career, Holly reminded herself. Staying at a luxury chalet in the Alps was a wonderful perk of her job. She took a chocolate from the dish on the coffee table and bit into it. The creamy truffle tasted divine, and she closed her eyes while she focused her senses on the sensual pleasure of the chocolate melting on her tongue.

'At least my sister is happy that I have decided to remain at the Frieden Clinic for the next few weeks.'

Holly's eyes flew open and she saw Jarek slip his phone into his pocket before he strolled over and sat down on the footstool close to her chair. Too close for her comfort, she thought, watching the firelight dance over his hair and throw the hard angles of his face into sharp relief. Her fingers literally *ached* to discover if the blond stubble shading his jaw felt prickly to the touch.

'Elin sounded nice when I spoke to her before you arrived...' she murmured, annoyed with herself for feeling pleased that his phone call had been from his sister. 'She told me that the orphanage where you lived in Sarajevo was partially destroyed when it was hit by mortar shells. Elin said she was too young for her to remember much about the war, but she knows that you took care of her and undoubtedly saved her life many times.'

He shrugged. 'I am six years older than my sister. There was no one else to look after her because many of the staff were killed. The kids who survived were the forgotten children of a brutal war,' he said grimly. 'When there was a lull in the machine gun fire I used to go out with a couple of other boys to steal food from the few shops that still operated. We'd take provisions back to the younger children in the orphanage.'

'It sounds horrific. What happened to your parents?'

'They died in a bomb explosion.' Jarek's voice

was emotionless. 'Apparently it was a miracle that Elin and I were pulled from the rubble alive.'

'It must have been devastating to lose your parents when you were so young,' Holly said softly. 'Do you remember much about them?'

'I don't have any memories of them.' His jaw clenched. 'I was told by the orphanage staff that the trauma of the explosion had somehow wiped out all my memories of my parents.' He stared at her with an odd intensity in his bright blue eyes. 'Is that possible? As far as I'm aware I did not suffer any head injury which could have caused memory loss.'

'Well, post-traumatic stress can be responsible for memory loss, but it is more likely to manifest with a person having flashbacks and nightmares of a traumatic experience,' Holly said thoughtfully. 'There is a form of memory loss called dissociative amnesia, in which information is lost from the conscious mind as a result of emotional trauma. In such cases a person's behaviour can be influenced by a past trauma, even though their conscious mind doesn't remember what happened. For instance, if a young girl was dragged into some bushes and raped, she might, as an adult, be terrified to walk through woodland. But because her mind has blocked out the rape she doesn't understand the reason for her fear.'

'Do you mean that the brain blocks out bad memories? I have sometimes wondered if I had an unhappy life with my parents, which is why I can't remember them.'

'I suppose that's possible. Another explanation might be that you had a loving relationship with your parents and losing them suddenly was so traumatic that you developed what can be described as emotional amnesia—meaning that you are unable to remember events which occurred in a specific period of time. That would explain why you have no memories of your life before your parents were killed. How much do you remember of living at the orphanage?'

'I remember *everything* about that hellhole.'

The harsh scrape of Jarek's voice sent a shiver through Holly.

'I'm thankful that my sister was too young to remember much.' He pushed his hair off his face. 'I can only think that whatever happened when I was very young must have been unimaginably horrific for my mind to have blocked out all early memories of my childhood, and yet I am able to recall vividly the terrible things I witnessed in Sarajevo.'

'I read in your notes that you have had an MRI scan which reveals no indication of any structural brain injury. That suggests that we should focus on psychological testing to try to get to the root of your memory loss. Psychotherapy and CBT—cognitive behaviour therapy—have both proved to be highly successful in helping patients to recover memory.'

'You must have heard the saying "Let sleeping dogs lie"? I can't help but think I should do the same,' Jarek murmured.

His lazy tone took Holly by surprise after the rawness she'd heard in his voice moments earlier. He smiled, but there was a bleakness in his eyes that tugged on her tender heart as she pictured him as a young orphaned boy, trapped in a besieged city during one of Europe's bloodiest civil wars.

'I believe your fear of what lies in the past will prevent you from finding happiness in the future.

I want to help you unlock your memories,' she told him softly.

His sharp gaze searched her face. 'Why?'

'I know what it's like at the bottom of the well...what it's like to be in a place so deep and dark that you can't imagine the light, let alone see it.' She swallowed, wondering why she had revealed her vulnerable side to Jarek. 'Besides, you're paying me a lot of money to be your psychotherapist,' she said briskly. 'And, actually, I am very good at what I do.'

'I'm sure you are.'

His voice turned smoky and curled around her, making her fiercely aware of him.

'Actually,' he mimicked gently, *'I* am very good at what I do, too.'

Holly flushed as she guessed he wasn't referring to his skill at studying the financial markets and making money. She hadn't noticed him move closer, but he was right there in front of her. The footstool he was sitting on was slightly lower than her chair, and his eyes were level with hers when he leaned forward and rested his forearms on the arms of the chair, caging her in. She felt her heart collide painfully with her ribs as he stretched out his hand and brushed his thumb over her lips.

The effect on her was dizzying. Scalding heat swept through her veins and pooled, molten and shockingly needy, between her legs. Somehow she resisted the temptation to part her lips and draw his thumb into her mouth. She wanted him inside her—in every way.

The startling realisation acted as a reminder that her body would fail her, as it had done so humiliatingly in the past.

She jerked her head away from him. 'What are you doing?'

'You had chocolate on your mouth.' He lifted his thumb to his own mouth and licked off the smear of chocolate that he had removed from her lips.

Heat rolled through her again and a curious heaviness filled her breasts and unfurled in the pit of her stomach. *This has to stop right now*, a sane voice in her head demanded. Amusement gleamed in Jarek's eyes, but there was also something darker and more intent that stole her breath. He was a notorious womaniser, she reminded herself, and she was way out of her depth.

But she could not seem to move…could not tear her eyes from his mouth as he leaned forward, bringing his face so near to hers that his warm breath grazed her lips.

He was going to kiss her.

Holly trembled, wanting to feel his mouth on hers more than she had ever wanted anything in her life. She swayed towards him, bringing their bodies so close that she could see the tiny lines around his eyes and the faintly calculating expression in his ice-blue gaze.

Unease rippled down her spine.

He was her *patient.*

The cool voice of her sanity spoke again, forcing her to acknowledge that she was in danger of throwing away everything she had worked so hard for. It was not just her professionalism she was risking but her dignity and self-respect. Had she been tempted to sacrifice all that? For what? A five-minute fumble with the tabloids' favourite bad-boy, she silently answered her own question.

'I think I'll go to bed,' she said jerkily, and silently cursed herself for sounding so gauche. She managed to restrain herself from adding the clarification *alone.*

Jarek lifted his brows as if he knew—damn him—the shockingly erotic images that flashed into her mind of them in bed together.

She swallowed. 'It's late.'

Following his gaze over to the clock, she steeled herself for him to point out in his lazy drawl that nine-thirty was hardly 'late'.

To her relief, he made no comment and did not try to stop her when she jumped up from her chair.

'Goodnight,' she choked. 'We'll start proper therapy tomorrow.'

His dry rejoinder, 'I'll look forward to it,' mocked her as she fled from the room.

CHAPTER FIVE

A LINE OF black limousines queued outside Salzburg's grandest hotel, waiting to deliver guests to the masquerade ball. Jarek tried to curb his impatience as Gunther inched the car slowly forward. He was not in any hurry to get to the ball—which he expected would be as tedious as such events usually were—but from as far back as he could remember he had felt an inexplicable sense of claustrophobia when he was in a car.

It was why he preferred to ride a motorbike.

He wondered if his irrational fear of travelling in cars was connected to his nightmares. Something Holly had said about it being possible for a forgotten trauma from the past to influence behaviour in adulthood had resonated with him.

This evening, when the chauffeur had opened the door for him to climb into the back of the car, he'd felt a sense of terror as a wisp of real memory or a bad dream—he did not know which—

had flashed into his head. It had faded before he could assimilate what he had seen, but it had shaken him.

He stared out of the window, watching the flurry of snowflakes drifting down from the night sky. If he had been on his own he would have jumped out onto the pavement and walked the last few hundred yards to the hotel's entrance. But the temperature outside was below zero and Holly would freeze in her strapless ballgown.

He could do with a blast of cold air to bring his temperature down, Jarek thought as he glanced at her sitting beside him. Desire kicked hard in his groin as he allowed his eyes to linger on the creamy upper slopes of her breasts, rising above the low-cut neckline of her dress.

'Explain to me why we are attending a masked ball,' he murmured, in an attempt to divert his mind from the erotic fantasies about her that had made him uncomfortably hard ever since she'd walked into the lounge at Chalet Soline, looking as if she belonged in an adults-only fairy tale, wearing a dramatic creation of burgundy silk and lace.

The dress's full skirt emphasised Holly's tiny

waist, and Jarek was sorely tempted to press his mouth against the smooth skin of her bare shoulder and kiss his way down to the deep valley between her breasts.

'Austria is famed for its ball season, which lasts from just before Christmas right through until early summer,' she told him. 'And Professor Heppel believes it is important for patients to attend social functions accompanied by their therapists, so that they can address any issues which might stem from social anxiety. For example, a person might drink heavily to boost their self-confidence. Although I very much doubt that a lack of confidence is the reason why *you* drink,' she said drily.

Jarek's mouth twitched. He was frequently amused by her acerbic wit, and greatly entertained by the way she bristled when he teased her. Holly's nature was as prickly as her name suggested, and he found her disapproval of him a novelty when other women invariably fawned on him.

He stretched his arm along the back of the car seat and was delighted when she stiffened. 'Are you saying that alcohol will be served at the ball?

Suddenly the evening promises to be more entertaining.'

She jerked her head round, and even in the dark interior of the car he felt the force of the glare she directed at him. 'Obviously you are expected to stay away from the bar. The point of the exercise is for you to understand that you do not need to get drunk in order to have a good time. I'll be keeping a close eye on you the entire evening,' she warned. 'In case you get any ideas.'

'Oh, I have *lots* of ideas.' He couldn't resist lowering his head so he could whisper in her ear. 'I am *very* inventive.'

He was fascinated by the scarlet stain that bloomed on her pretty face. Her blush spread down her throat and across the slopes of her magnificent breasts, which reminded him of ripe peaches that he longed to taste.

'You have to stop this,' she snapped. 'It is completely inappropriate for you to flirt with your psychologist. Or at least I'm *supposed* to be giving you therapy,' she muttered, her frustration evident in her voice. 'But you have been at Chalet Soline for a week and we have only managed one half-hour session.'

'I don't know *where* the week has gone,' he said blandly.

'You seem to have spent most of it sleeping.' The bite in her tone was even sharper. 'I've never known a man to lounge around in bed like you do.'

'Have you known *many* men?'

Behind his teasing he realised that he really wanted to know—which was curious, because he had never been mildly interested in his mistresses' tally of lovers. But, despite the simmering sexual chemistry between him and Holly, he could *not* risk making her his mistress, Jarek brooded.

The realisation that he liked her as well as desired her made him even more determined to resist her. Nothing good ever came to the people he cared about. Holly wanted him to confide his darkest secrets to her, but if he did that she would run as fast and as far from him as she could get—if she had any sense.

'My love-life is none of your business.'

She tightened her fingers around her evening purse, and Jarek had an idea that she was imagining she had her hands around his throat.

'Seriously, every day last week you only emerged from your bedroom at lunchtime, and every afternoon you took yourself off to the Frieden Clinic's treatment centre for a massage. I don't suppose it has anything to do with the fact that the Swedish masseuse, Inga, is a very attractive blonde?' she suggested sarcastically.

Her voice softened.

'Don't think I haven't realised that you are avoiding me, Jarek. It's not unusual for people embarking on psychological treatment to find talking about their problems difficult to begin with.'

The way she spoke his name felt like a kick in his gut. He wanted to pull the pins from her elegant chignon and thread his fingers through her mass of silky brown hair. Worse, he wanted to tell her things he had never told anyone else— not even his sister.

He could not risk upsetting Elin with his crazy idea that their parents *hadn't* died in a bomb blast in Sarajevo, as they had always believed.

In the past week there had been further media reports on the rumour circulating in the Principality of Vostov that the royal family had been assassinated two decades ago, on the orders of a military commander. Ordinarily Jarek would not have taken much interest in the story, but the letter he'd received a few weeks ago, and the request for him to have a DNA test, were preying on his mind.

'Who is Tarik?' Holly asked quietly, jolting him from his thoughts. 'I heard you shout out the name in the middle of the night. Your bedroom is at the opposite end of the chalet from mine, so you must have been shouting loudly to have woken me. Did you have a nightmare?'

'If I did I don't remember it,' he lied.

The dream was one he'd had many times before: a car standing on a driveway with its engine running, bright headlamps cutting white circles in the dark night. People talking in frantic voices. He sensed their fear, but in his dream he could not see their faces. Someone was trying to bundle him into the car but he didn't want to go, and he was crying, shouting out a name.

Tarik...

'You have no idea who Tarik is?' she persisted. 'He might be the key to unlocking your lost memories.'

He looked away from her searching gaze. 'Actually, I remember that Tarik was a boy I knew at the orphanage. We used to play football when the bombing stopped for a while.'

His answer seemed to satisfy Holly. But Jarek knew that the boy in the orphanage had been called Ivan. Years after he had been adopted by the Saundersons he had returned to Sarajevo, to see if any of his friends had survived. He'd found Ivan living rough on the streets—a drug addict and as much a victim of the war as the thousands of people who had perished at the time.

Jarek knew that *he* could have been Ivan, but by a twist of fate he had been taken to live at a stately home—Cuckmere Hall in England. His sense of guilt that he had escaped the hell of war when so many like Ivan had not added to the weight of guilt on his shoulders. Lorna Saunderson had rescued him from the orphanage and been a mother to him. But he had repaid her kindness with reckless behaviour that had cost Mama her life.

He was glad to escape his thoughts as the car came to a halt in front of the entrance to the hotel.

But his relief was short-lived when he noticed the bright glare of a camera flashbulb.

'You didn't mention that the goddamned press would be here,' he accused Holly.

A picture in the newspapers of him arriving at the ball would alert Vostov's National Council that he was in Austria.

'The photographer doesn't work for the press. He is simply taking photos of people as they arrive. The guests will be able to buy the pictures to raise funds for the children's charity the ball is in aid of. I know you promised your brother-in-law that you would keep a low profile until your sister has her baby, but I doubt the paparazzi will be interested in a charity ball in Salzburg,' Holly murmured. 'Anyway, your mask will hide your identity.'

She handed him a black eye mask before affixing her own over her face. Her mask was an elaborate affair, decorated with sparkling diamante and feathers which drew attention to her big brown eyes. A man could drown in those velvet-soft eyes if he wasn't careful, Jarek brooded as he stepped out of the car.

He offered her his arm to escort her into the

hotel and noted how she hesitated and took a deep breath that caused her breasts to rise and fall before she placed her hand on his arm.

The hotel's foyer was crowded with guests: the women were wearing elaborate ballgowns and the men resplendent in tuxedos. Double doors opened onto the ballroom, which was ablaze with lights from crystal chandeliers.

'We don't have to stay here.' Holly spoke in an undertone as they walked into the ballroom. 'In the car I felt that you were finally starting to open up when you spoke about your childhood friend Tarik, from the orphanage. I think we should go back to Chalet Soline to discuss the parts of your childhood that you do remember. There may be something that triggers memories of your parents.'

Jarek kept his expression bland. He had deliberately made himself unavailable for therapy sessions all week—which was undoubtedly the act of a coward, he acknowledged grimly. But his strategy of avoiding being alone with Holly was under threat. At least while they were at the ball there would be no chance of the soul-searching conversation she was so keen on.

And so he gave her one of the easy smiles that he'd learned as a teenager never failed to win women over. Desire jack-knifed inside him as he watched her pupils dilate, so that the eyes staring at him from behind her mask darkened with a sultry promise he knew he would ultimately have to resist.

'It would be a pity to leave now that we are here—especially when you are the belle of the ball. You look stunning in your ballgown,' he murmured.

It was not an idle compliment. Her lovely face and gorgeous figure evoked an odd tightness in his chest, and a rather more predictable tightening in his groin.

'Working on uncovering my past can wait until another day.' *Preferably another millennium*, Jarek thought to himself. 'Tonight I'd much rather focus on the present.'

The orchestra struck up a waltz and he swept her into his arms before she could argue.

As he steered Holly around the dance floor Jarek was grateful to his adoptive mother for teaching him the social graces that had allowed him to fit in with high society. He had been a feral boy who had lived off his wits to survive in a war when Lorna Saunderson had persuaded her husband to adopt him. Now, at this grand ball, he suddenly felt an odd sense of recognition.

A memory flashed into his mind. He saw himself as a child, sitting at the top of a wide staircase and peering down through the banisters on a huge room below. There was a crowd of people dressed in ornate clothes, and he could hear music and the indistinct buzz of chatter and laughter. It must have been a party, but Jarek sensed it had not taken place in Sarajevo. Where could he have been when he had observed such revelry from his secret hiding place? And where had his parents been?

Holly had suggested that thinking about his childhood might trigger memories of his parents, but Jarek could not picture them. It was as if a curtain had been pulled across his past and he feared what he might discover if he tried to see behind it.

He needed a distraction, and previously vodka had provided a welcome escape from his demons. But if he went anywhere near the bar tonight his personal gaoler would be right beside him to give him one of her pithy lectures.

That left him with only one option, he brooded as he tightened his arm around Holly's waist and pulled her hard up against his body. He would have to distract himself with his beautiful psychotherapist.

Holly ran the zip of her dress down her spine and dragged in a deep breath, relieved finally to be able to fill her lungs with oxygen. The ballgown's boned bodice emphasised her narrow waist and pushed her breasts high, but after several hours of having her ribcage constricted she was glad to change into comfortable cotton pyjamas.

Not that she felt like sleeping. It was past midnight, and she should be tired after she'd danced the night away with Jarek at the ball. But her heart was still racing as fast as it had been when he'd whisked her around the ballroom. She had felt giddy as he'd held her—so close to him that she'd felt his powerful thighs pressed up against her. At some point she had given up trying to hold herself stiffly and had melted into him, unable to resist the sexual chemistry that had burned like a white-hot flame between them.

It had been a magical evening. But reality had caught up with her when Gunther had driven them back to Chalet Soline after the ball had finished. In the car Jarek had seemed tense and uncommunicative—in marked contrast to his behaviour throughout the evening, when he had been so charming and attentive that Holly admitted she had fallen under his spell.

Back at the chalet, the chef had left a tray of coffee in the sitting room, where the embers of the fire had emitted a welcoming glow. She had half-expected Jarek to suggest they drink their coffee together, but he had bade her a curt goodnight and gone straight up to his bedroom, leaving her feeling deflated and rather stupid.

What had she hoped might happen if they'd sat in the cosy sitting room with the lights turned down low? she angrily asked her reflection as she pulled the pins out of her chignon and dug her fingers into her hair to massage her scalp. The evening could not have ended any differently even if Jarek *hadn't* been her patient.

She opened her bedside drawer and took out

the purse that contained her set of dilators. The surgery she'd had as a teenager had been successful in lengthening her vagina, but her gynaecologist had advised her to use the dilators a few times a month if she wasn't having sex regularly. After Stuart had ended their relationship a year ago Holly had not dated anyone seriously. She'd continued to use her dilators, but not as often as she knew she should—because there didn't seem much point when she seemed destined to remain single.

Logically, she knew she shouldn't feel ashamed or embarrassed about her body, but a little voice inside her head whispered that Jarek could have any woman he wanted, and was unlikely to want *her* if he found out that she was a freak.

She shoved the dilators back in the drawer before she climbed into bed and then opened her notebook to write up Jarek's notes. She had a job to do, she reminded herself fiercely. She'd been an idiot to fall for his seduction routine at the ball—which, quite clearly, had been a calculated ploy to stop her from delving into his emotions. But behind Jarek's image of indolent playboy— an image she was beginning to realise he cultivated deliberately—she'd glimpsed the damaged soul of a boy who had witnessed the horrors of war and risked his life to protect his younger sister when he had been only a child.

Holly knew that severe childhood trauma could have a lasting and devastating effect throughout a person's life, and even though Jarek did not want her help she would nevertheless do her best to persuade him to start a programme of counselling sessions. Tomorrow she would not let him out of her sight, she resolved as she curled up beneath the duvet and turned off the bedside lamp.

She woke with a start and felt disorientated to find herself in darkness. She had been dreaming that she was in a brightly lit ballroom. Her brain caught up and remembered that she was in her bedroom at Chalet Soline, and when she switched on the lamp she saw on the clock that it was four in the morning. Dawn was still three hours or so away, and while she was wondering what had woken her she heard Jarek's voice.

He was shouting, as he had done the previous night—harsh, incomprehensible words. Dear God, the fear in his voice tore on Holly's heart. What terrors stalked his nightmares?

She threw back the covers and leapt out of bed, driven by an instinctive desire to help him. She did not even pause to grab her robe before she ran down the corridor to his room.

The first thing she noticed when she opened his bedroom door was a table by the window, upon which three brightly lit computer monitors displayed columns of red and green numbers.

'Jarek?' she called softly.

He did not reply, and while she hovered in the doorway, wondering if she should return to her room, he cried out again, and the tortured sound sent a shiver through her. The glow from the computer screens allowed her to make out his shape on the bed. She walked over to him and, after hesitating for a second, switched on the bed-side lamp and saw that he was sprawled on top of the bedspread.

His tuxedo jacket, she noticed, was draped over the back of a chair. He was still wearing his trousers, and his white silk shirt was unbuttoned so that it hung open to reveal a muscular chest covered with whorls of dark blond hair. Holly dared not allow her eyes to travel over his flat abdomen and lower, to where the path of body hair disappeared beneath his waistband. Instead she forced her gaze up to his face, and was struck anew by the stark beauty of his hard-boned features.

One arm was lying across his eyes. Holly's heart twisted when she saw a single tear slide down his cheek.

'Jarek!' she said more loudly, desperate to rouse him from his nightmare.

She leaned over the bed and gave a startled cry when his eyes flew open and he snapped his fingers around her wrist. He gave a hard tug, so that without quite knowing how she ended up sitting on the edge of the bed, next to where he lay.

'Is this an example of your bedside manner, Dr Maitland?' he drawled. 'I usually wear nothing in bed… There could have been an interesting development in our patient/psychologist relationship if you'd sneaked into my bedroom and found me stark naked.'

Amusement gleamed in his bright blue eyes when she blushed, and Holly's sympathy for him was replaced by a desire to slap the smug grin off his face.

'I did *not* sneak into your room,' she said tightly. 'You must have been having a nightmare—you were shouting. You woke me up.' She tried to no avail to tug her wrist out of his grasp. 'I came to see if I could help. You said the name Tarik again, but I couldn't understand anything else because you were speaking in a language I didn't recognise.'

'My first language is Bosnian,' Jarek said slowly. He sat up and leaned against the headboard of the bed, still retaining his hold on her wrist. The teasing smile that had played on his lips a few seconds earlier had disappeared. 'I rarely spoke it after I was adopted and learned to speak English. My sister was too young to remember any of the Bosnian language.'

'The fact that you called out in your first language suggests you were dreaming about an incident in your childhood. Can you remember anything about the dream?' Holly pressed.

'No. But the recent volatility of the financial markets is enough to give *anyone* nightmares,' he quipped.

'I don't think your dream was about tumbling share prices on the stockmarket.' She swallowed her frustration and looked over at the blinking computer monitors. 'Why is your computer system active at this time of night? Well, technically it's four-thirty in the morning, but it feels like the middle of the night to *me*.'

Jarek pushed his untidy blond hair off his face. 'I had been working before I sat on the bed for a couple of minutes. I must have fallen asleep.'

'Working?' Holly could not hide her surprise. 'I know you said you wanted to use the study downstairs as your office, but every time I've walked passed that room you haven't been there, and I've never actually seen you do any work.'

'I don't make vast amounts of money by sitting around and twiddling my thumbs,' he said drily. 'Of *course* I work. Mainly at night, because most of my trading is on the financial markets in the Far East, which is on a different time zone to Europe. One a.m. here is nine a.m. in places like Hong Kong and Shanghai, when the Asian stock exchanges are open for trading.'

'So you have to catch up on sleep in the day-time to make up for the fact that you stay awake working most of the night...' Holly stared at him. 'Why do you encourage the media to portray you as a feckless playboy?'

He gave another shrug. 'How do you know that I'm not *exactly* as I'm perceived by the press?'

'I looked you up on the internet,' she admitted. 'Amid the countless stories of your wild womanising and partying, which seem to confirm your bad-boy reputation, I discovered just how much money you have raised for the charity Lorna's Gift. Another little-known fact overlooked by the press is that you spend several months every year visiting orphanages around the world. You are the driving force behind a scheme in some of the world's poorer countries to promote the idea that it is better for children who have no families of their own to be fostered rather than grow up in institutions.'

'Don't make me out as some kind of saint,' Jarek told her harshly. 'The truth is that there's not much difference between financial trading and gambling. I take big risks, and I've been lucky so far that most have paid off. But that wasn't the case two years ago, when I caused the near-collapse of Saunderson's Bank.' He gave a bitter laugh. 'My adoptive father was right when he said I have a destructive streak in my nature.'

'I don't believe that is true.' Holly looked away

from him and quickly blinked away the tears that welled in her eyes. Jarek sounded so *raw*. 'I wish you would allow me to try and help you,' she said in a low tone. 'Regression therapy might enable you to relive a traumatic event from your past, so that you can come to terms with whatever happened to you when you were a child.'

'You have a soft heart, don't you, angel-face?'

His voice was deeper than Holly had ever heard it, and if her heart hadn't already melted it would have done then.

'You should have told me to leave Chalet Soline when you had the chance—and when I stood a chance of resisting you,' he told her. 'But now it's too late.'

She swallowed as he picked up a lock of her long hair and wound it around his fingers. The intent expression in his eyes caused her heart to slam into her ribs, and she knew he must be able to feel the erratic thud of her pulse as he stroked his thumb-pad over her wrist.

'I'm not a fool,' she told him stiffly. 'At the ball tonight you pretended to be attracted to me to distract me from asking awkward questions which might reveal something about your past.'

'Is that what you think I was doing?'

'I *know* it was. When we returned to the chalet you couldn't wait to get away from me.'

'What do you think would have happened, Holly?' he murmured. 'If we had been alone in the sitting room, with the flames crackling in the hearth and both of us imagining making love on the fur rug in front of the fire?'

Betraying colour flooded her face as she recalled her erotic fantasy. It had been exactly as Jarek had described. 'I wasn't imagining anything of the sort,' she denied jerkily.

'Liar!'

His laughter was a soft rumble that tugged at something deep inside her. Her breath caught in her throat when he gave a little tug on her hair to pull her head nearer to his. Like a fish caught on a hook, she thought, except that she didn't try to escape as he reeled her in.

She licked her dry lips, unable to look away from his glittering blue gaze as he drew her closer to him, closer to the wickedly sensual mouth that crooked in a knowing smile.

'What are you doing?' she demanded in a husky voice she did not recognise as her own.

'What you want me to do,' he promised.

His arrogance should have appalled her. But Holly was beyond caring about anything other than her desperate need for him to kiss her. Time was suspended, and she had the crazy feeling that she had been waiting for this moment and for this man her whole life. She could feel her heart trying to claw its way out of her chest as Jarek's breath whispered across her lips. He angled his mouth over hers. And then he simply claimed her—as if he was her master and she belonged utterly and entirely to him.

His kiss was everything she had imagined it would be. Hot, hungry, demanding her response. And she was powerless to deny him. She went up in flames instantly, and in a distant recess of her mind she recognised that she had never been kissed so expertly before.

Jarek was the Viking invader of her fantasies about him, and his kiss was no gentle seduction but a passionate plundering of her senses. He used his tongue with consummate skill to explore her mouth and thrust his hand into her hair to hold her prisoner while he kissed her with a stunning eroticism that made her tremble.

He finally let go of her wrist—but only so that he could wrap his arms around her and haul her against his bare chest. Her hands flailed wildly for a second, before she succumbed to temptation and placed them flat on his chest, running her fingers over the whorls of blond hair that grew thickly over his torso. She pushed his unbuttoned shirt off his shoulders and revelled in the feel of his satin-smooth skin beneath her palms. His body was a masterpiece of masculine beauty and she traced her fingers over the hard ridges of his abdominal muscles, fascinated by his toned hardness in contrast to her soft, feminine curves.

In a seamless movement he rolled her over, so that she found herself lying on her back on the bed. He stretched out beside her and propped himself up on his elbow, cradling her chin in his other hand while he kissed her again, slow and leisurely this time, but no less heart-shaking.

Holly ran her fingers through his hair. Her senses were inflamed by the heat of his body, the musky fragrance of his aftershave and the skilful flick of his tongue inside her mouth. She sank deeper into the soft mattress as he smoothed his hand down her body, over the firm mounds of her breasts covered by the stretchy material of her pyjama top. Her heart thudded when he gripped the hem of her top and in one fluid movement pushed it up to her neck, baring her breasts. The cool air on her heated skin caused her nipples to pucker, and the feral growl Jarek gave sent a shudder of response through her.

'Your breasts are even more beautiful than I had imagined them,' he said thickly. 'I wish that I had followed my instincts when we returned from the ball, and undressed you in the firelight before making love to you in front of the fire.'

The sound of his voice jolted Holly from the sexual haze that had clouded her brain. The inherent arrogance of his statement sent a chill through her.

'Assuming I would have *allowed* you to undress me,' she muttered.

'Of course you would.'

He laughed, and it felt like a knife through her heart.

'Why *else* did you come to my room tonight?'

'You were having a nightmare.' She yanked her pyjama top down and sat up. 'You *can't* think I came for any other reason?' Her face flamed when he looked amused. 'I am your psychotherapist and I rushed to your room after I heard you call out to see if I could help you.' She gave a ragged sigh of frustration. 'The truth is that we can't start a relationship while you are my client.'

'Relationship?' His brows rose. 'I thought we were going to spend what's left of the night together—not align our diaries for the next few months.'

Holly welcomed the burst of temper that exploded inside her and which—for now, at least—stopped her feeling as if she wanted to cry. What a fool she was, she thought grimly.

'I suppose the thought of being with a woman for even one month must seem like an eternity to the world's most prolific playboy,' she said furiously. 'You shouldn't have kissed me, and I admit I should not have responded. It was a moment of madness and I assure you it won't happen again.'

She swung her legs over the side of the bed and stood up, telling herself she was relieved that he did not try to stop her. To her utter shame she smelled the betraying musky scent of her arousal, and was sure Jarek must be able to smell it too.

It was no wonder that he had assumed she was his for the taking.

But if he had attempted to have sex with her he would have found her body unyielding, and she would have felt even more humiliated than she did right now.

Feeling sick with self-loathing, she hurried over to the door. But she hesitated on her way out of his room and turned to face him. He was still sprawled on the bed, like an indolent sultan deciding which of the concubines in his harem he would summon to pleasure him.

For a mad moment Holly wondered what would happen if she forgot her principles and walked back over to him, peeling off her pyjamas on her way to his bed. Her breasts ached for his touch, and there was a slick, molten heat between her legs. But the fantasy was ruined by the reality that it took time for her body to become fully aroused, and that if she rushed sex would be uncomfortable for her.

'When I heard you shouting you sounded terrified—as if someone was trying to murder you,' she told Jarek. 'You are going to have to confront your past some time—and, although I feel hor-

ribly embarrassed about my unprofessional behaviour tonight, I want you to know that my only
desire is to help you tackle your demons.'

For a split second an expression flashed across
his face that startled Holly. He looked *lost*—and
vulnerable, as he must have been when he was
an orphaned boy struggling to survive in war-
torn Sarajevo.

Her heart ached for him, but he wasn't interested in her heart, she reminded herself as she
stepped into the corridor and quietly closed the
door behind her.

CHAPTER SIX

'I'M GLAD TO see you've made it down to breakfast for once,' Holly said, coming to an abrupt halt in the doorway of the dining room when she saw Jarek sitting at the table, drinking a cup of coffee.

She did not sound gladdened by the sight of him, he thought. Her usually melodious voice was at least two octaves higher, and the pink stain on her cheeks reminded him of when he had shoved her pyjama top out of the way and watched warm colour spread down her throat and over her perfect round breasts with their rosy tips that he had ached to taste.

He still ached, he acknowledged. Sleepless nights were nothing new to him, but since Holly had left him last night he'd felt restless and dangerously out of control. Unexpectedly he'd found he wanted something more than the litany of meaningless liaisons that defined his life. But he should know better. He knew himself too well, and none of what he knew was any good.

The headlines on many of the morning's newspapers did not help to lighten Jarek's mood.

In Vostov, Asmir Sunjic had gone public with his story that he had been in the car with Prince Goran and his wife and children on the night of the fatal crash that had supposedly taken the lives of every member of the royal family. Asmir insisted that the crash had not been the result of a tyre blow-out, as had been reported at the time, but that in fact the car had been hit by gunfire. Even more astonishing was Asmir's claim that when the car had spun off the road and crashed into dense woodland he had managed to smuggle the royal children away to safety. Moments later the car had exploded in a fireball, with the Prince and Princess inside.

If the old Vostovian man's story was true, the papers suggested, the royal children—who would now be adults—might be alive.

It was a big *if*, Jarek brooded. He welcomed the distraction of watching Holly walk across the room and take her place opposite him at the table. Her colour was still high, and he was intrigued when she refused to meet his gaze and seemed to be fascinated with the toast rack.

'I've drawn up a schedule of counselling sessions for you,' she said, in a brisk tone that warned him she would not be distracted from her determination to persuade him to spill his guts. She was dressed as if she meant business, but he knew that her calf-length skirt and crisp blouse—buttoned all the way up to her neck this morning—concealed a voluptuous body. He felt himself harden as he recalled how soft her sweet curves had felt when he'd held her in his arms.

'How very efficient of you,' he drawled.

He was tempted to reach across the table and remove the clasp that secured her hair in a knot on top of her head, so that the heavy mass of gleaming brown silk spilled around her shoulders. But if he did that he knew he would have to walk around the table and sink his fingers into her hair, so he contented himself with brushing his fingertips over the faint grazes on her cheek.

'I left my mark on you last night,' he said ruefully, rubbing his hand across the stubble on his jaw. 'Perhaps it's as well that things did not progress between us. Your skin is so fine that if I had put my mouth on your breasts I would have scraped you with my beard.'

She stiffened, and he waited for her to slap him down with one of her sharp retorts. Instead her silence trembled with tension, and Jarek felt an odd sensation as if his heart was being squeezed in a vice when he saw her lower lip wobble before she caught it between her teeth.

'You don't need to remind me of my shameful behaviour last night.' Her voice shook. 'I will understand if you wish to make a complaint about my unprofessional conduct to Professor Heppel.'

Even worse than the painful emotion in her voice was the dark luminosity of her eyes. 'For God's sake, Holly,' he said roughly, 'there is no reason for you to feel ashamed. Believe me, I should know. Shame is my middle name.'

'I wonder why you think that. It will be a good starting point for your first counselling session.' The determined look was back in her eyes. 'I thought we could make a start straight after breakfast.'

For twenty seconds Jarek considered telling Holly of his crazy suspicion that his amnesia about the early years of his life was somehow connected with events that had taken place in the Principality of Vostov more than two decades ago. But he was sure she would not believe him—and he did not really believe himself that Asmir Sunjic's story could be true. If his parents had been a prince and princess, it seemed inconceivable that he had no memory of them—or of spending the first years of his childhood living in a royal palace.

How, then, had he ended up in an orphanage in Sarajevo? There were so many unanswered questions. It was more likely that the old man in Vostov was a fantasist, or an opportunist hoping to make money by selling his bizarre story to the media, Jarek assured himself.

He glanced at Holly and found her watching him with big dark eyes that reminded him of molten chocolate: soft and sweet and so very tempting.

'I've decided to go skiing this morning,' he said abruptly. 'Heavy snowfall is forecast for the next few days, which means that today might be the only opportunity to hit the slopes.'

She looked as if she wanted to argue, but perhaps she guessed it would be pointless because she murmured, 'All right. I'll come with you. Maybe spending the day outside in the fresh air will help you to relax and you'll feel able to talk about your childhood.'

'How can I talk about it when a chunk of my memory is missing?' he growled irritably. 'You make it sound simple, but presumably the reason my mind has blocked out certain memories is because they are disturbing.'

She nodded. 'But your lost memories surface in your nightmares. Whatever happened to you as a child is stored in your subconscious mind.'

'What the hell is wrong with leaving those memories buried, instead of digging them up so that you can psychoanalyse them?' he demanded, feeling that restless ache inside him when she smiled gently.

'I hope I can help you to uncover your past so that you will be freed from the horrors that stalk your dreams.'

'What if *I* am the horror?' he muttered. 'What if I am afraid to remember my early childhood because I did something terrible?'

He saw her shocked expression before she

quickly masked it. What had made him blurt out his secret fear to Holly, Jarek wondered grimly.

She shook her head. 'How old were you when you went to live at the orphanage and were told that your parents had died?

'Six. But I have no memories of my life up until then.'

'You were a *child*, Jarek,' she said softly. 'What can a six-year-old boy have done?'

Killed his parents.

The thought flashed into Jarek's mind, along with that wisp of a memory he had seen before in his nightmares. He visualised a car with its engine running, heard a man's voice speaking urgently.

'Put the boy in the car, Dora. There is no time to search for Tarik. If we do not leave now we will all be killed.'

Who were Dora and Tarik? Jarek wondered. And why did he feel that he had somehow been responsible for his parents' death if they had been killed in a bomb explosion in Sarajevo?

Frustration surged through him when a curtain fell across his mind once more and hid his memories. His inability to recall his childhood was something he'd had to live with all his adult life, but he realised that Holly had been right when she'd said he could not look to the future until he had dealt with his past. Before he'd arrived at the Frieden Clinic and met his beautiful psycho-therapist he had been uninterested in what his future held. So why did it suddenly matter now?

He glanced at Holly and his jaw clenched. He shouldn't have kissed her, but now that he had he found himself wanting things he could never have. After his adoptive mother's death four years ago he had vowed that no one else would suffer as a result of his destructive nature.

Too restless to remain inactive, he scraped his chair back and rose to his feet. The gentle expres-sion in Holly's eyes felt like a knife in his heart. He did not need her sympathy and he was cer-tain he did not deserve it.

'How well can you ski?' he asked tersely. 'There are a couple of black runs at Arlenwald that I want to try, but if you are a novice you won't manage them. I'll leave you on the easier slopes.'

'As a matter of fact I'm an experienced skier. I was taught by an ex-boyfriend who was a skiing champion. Brett had an *amazing* technique,' she murmured, a smile playing on her lips.

He must be losing his mind, Jarek decided. What other reason could there be other than madness for the acid burn of jealousy in the pit of his stomach when he pictured Holly with another man?

'You said your skiing instructor was an ex-boyfriend... Was the break-up a recent event?'

She shook her head. 'No, I dated Brett years ago—while I was at university and working part-time as a model. We met at a party and he invited me to his home in Colorado, which is where I learned to ski. The romance fizzled out after a few months, but I've continued to ski regularly—mainly in Europe.'

'Why don't you have a man in your life currently?' Jarek hoped his idle tone disguised his curiosity.

'What makes you think I'm not in a relationship?' she countered.

'You wouldn't have kissed me if you were involved with another guy.'

He did not know why he was so certain that Holly was a one-man woman, but it was a reminder that she was off-limits to him. He sensed that he could hurt her. What was surprising was that he *cared*.

He watched her eyes darken and knew she was remembering the heat that had burned hotter than the fiercest flame between them when he had kissed her, and when she had responded with a sweet ardency that made his gut clench just thinking about it.

'I thought we had agreed that what happened last night was a mistake best forgotten,' she said tautly.

'I don't remember agreeing to forget it,' he drawled. 'Seriously, not only are you beautiful, but you are clever and compassionate—you must have to fight men off. I don't understand why you're not married.'

'That's rich, coming from a notorious playboy,' she murmured, in that dry way of hers that so amused Jarek.

He shrugged. 'I'm shallow and easily bored. What's your excuse?'

She was silent for a moment, and when she finally spoke the huskiness in her voice scraped on something raw inside him that he hadn't known existed until then.

'The truth is that I have never met anyone who was prepared to love me for the way I am,' she said quietly.

He frowned. 'And how *are* you?'

'Flawed.' She smiled faintly. 'You are not the only one with secrets, Jarek.'

'I'll tell you mine if you tell me yours.' He meant it, and it was then that he realised he was in grave danger of losing his sanity around Holly.

'I'm afraid that's not how psychotherapy works.' Her tone became brisk once more. 'It's only fair that if we spend today skiing you agree to give counselling a fair chance tomorrow.'

He couldn't help but smile at her earnest expression, and his smile widened as he walked around the table and bent his head down to hers. She immediately stiffened, and the pulse at the base of the throat leapt frantically beneath her skin.

'You're forgetting something, angel-face,' he said softly as he angled his mouth over hers.

The kiss was hard and fierce and unsatisfactorily brief. Desire delivered a sharp kick to his gut when he felt her lips part beneath his, and it took all his will power to lift his head and step away from her.

'I've never claimed to play fair.'

His voice was harsher than he'd intended: a warning to himself as much as to Holly, Jarek acknowledged as he spun round and strode out of the room.

The view down the mountainside was spectacular and terrifying. Holly felt a trickle of fear run the length of her spine as she stared at what appeared to be an almost vertical expanse of white snow, glistening in the late-afternoon sunshine. She had never attempted to ski down such a steep run before—although technically it wasn't a proper ski run.

Jarek had decided to ski off-piste, and she had felt that it was her duty to accompany him. The snow here, away from the main ski runs, had not been compacted by snowcat machines to flatten out the surface, and there were no coloured marker flags. More importantly there were no other skiers in sight—probably because no one else was crazy enough to want to ski on such challenging terrain.

She must be out of her mind, Holly thought, conscious of her heart hammering in her chest. Although she had told Jarek the truth when she'd said she was an experienced skier, she had omitted to mention that prior to arriving in Austria she had not skied for more than a year. The two black runs at Arlenwald were notoriously difficult, and her nerve and skill had been tested when she had followed Jarek down the slopes.

She had been feeling rather pleased with herself, and looking forward to a soak in the hot tub, knowing her muscles were going to ache like mad tomorrow— But...

'I'm not ready to finish yet,' Jarek had said when she'd suggested they return to Chalet Soline. 'You go back if you want to. I'll meet you later.'

'The daylight will fade soon,' she'd pointed out, but he had dismissed her argument and joined the queue for the ski lift, insisting there was enough time left for a final turn on the slopes.

'Call Gunther and ask him to drive you back to the chalet. I don't need a nursemaid.'

He had not hidden his irritation when she'd voiced her concern that it was dangerous to ski off-piste alone.

In fact Holly had not been worried about his physical safety. She'd quickly discovered that he was brilliant on skis—although he took too many risks, in her opinion. She was more concerned that if she left Jarek on the slopes he would be tempted to visit a bar back at the ski resort in order to enjoy the lively après-ski scene, thereby avoiding any in-depth conversation with her, as he had successfully been doing all day.

Her hope that when they took a break from skiing for lunch she would be able to encourage Jarek to talk about his childhood had been thwarted when he'd turned on his effortless charm. The memory of when he had kissed her at breakfast had weakened her resistance to him, and she had found herself responding to his outrageously sexy smile and entertaining conversation—even though she had known his deliberate seduction was a ploy to distract her from asking him questions about his past.

She was getting nowhere with Jarek's treatment, and Holly felt half inclined to give up with him. It was *not* part of her remit to chase him down a mountain, and she could not force him to have psychotherapy. But she couldn't forget the raw pain she had heard in his voice when she'd heard him shouting out in the night.

Clearly Jarek was haunted by the horrors of war that he had witnessed as a child, and he could not run from his past for ever, however much he tried, she brooded as she glanced at him, standing beside her at the top of the ski run. He had told her that he loved the mountains, but admitted that he did not remember where he had learned to ski. It was yet another mystery that she wanted to help him solve, if only he would let her.

She consoled herself with the thought that once they reached the bottom of the slope dusk would not be far off and they would not be able to ski any more that day. All she had to do was keep upright on her skis and pray that her nerve held on this final run.

'Are you sure you want to do this?' Jarek lifted up his goggles and scrutinised her face. 'You look nervous. It's fine if you want to chicken out.'

Her chin came up. His arrogance infuriated her, but she smiled sweetly and imagined him skiing over the edge of a ravine. 'I'm ready when you are.'

'Good.' He pulled his goggles back down over his eyes. 'Let's go.'

Jarek pushed off on his skis and was almost instantly engulfed by a cloud of powdery snow. Holly took a deep breath as she prepared to follow him.

The snow was deeper than she'd expected, and every time she turned snow flew up around her so that she could barely see ahead through the white cloud. She knew that on powder snow it was better to ski fast and establish a rhythm of short, even turns. It was exhilarating, and exhausting, but she dared not slow her pace because she could just see Jarek ahead, speeding away from her.

She concentrated on trying to catch up with him, and did not pay much attention when she heard an odd muffled sound. But moments later she noticed the snow around her starting to break away, and she knew—although she had never experienced it before—that a moving slab of snow was the first sign of an avalanche.

Terrified, Holly pointed her skis straight, desperately hoping she could outrun the avalanche, but then she heard a loud noise and saw a fracture line run across the snow slab as it shattered. Blocks of snow immediately started to slide down the mountain at an incredible speed. It felt as if a rug had been pulled from beneath her, and when she turned her head she saw that the entire side of the mountain had broken away and was hurtling down, ready to take her with it.

'Jarek!'

Through the cloud of white snow surrounding her she glimpsed his helmet, but she did not know if he had heard her voice. Her heart was pounding with fear as she fought to stay upright on her skis, aware that if she fell she would be swept down the mountainside and buried beneath tons of snow. She saw Jarek look over his shoulder and then point his ski stick over to a group of pine trees.

Holly turned her skis in the direction of the trees, adrenalin and a fierce instinct to survive sharpening her sense of balance as the snow slab beneath her skis swept her relentlessly down the mountain.

Somehow she managed to stay ahead of the

line of fast-moving snow until she reached the trees, and she grabbed hold of a branch just as the avalanche slammed into her. The snow still looked pretty and powdery, but it felt like a concrete wall hitting her. And it kept on coming—great slabs of snow crashing down, so that she had to cling to the branch with all her strength and pray that the tree would not be swept away by the tidal wave of snow, taking her with it to almost certain death.

Holly had no idea what had happened to Jarek, and before she could call out to him again a huge slab of snow smashed into her with such force that it felt as if her shoulder had been ripped out of its socket. The pain was indescribable, but she knew that if she fainted she would die, so somehow clung on to the tree branch for what seemed like a lifetime. Until miraculously the roaring noise that filled her ears abated and she realised the avalanche had stopped.

The sudden silence was eerie. Gradually she became aware of a ragged, uneven sound that she realised was her own shallow breathing. So she was alive. But she was unable to move because she discovered that she was buried up to her waist in snow, which was already setting like concrete. If she hadn't clung on to the branch of the tree Holly knew that she would have been completely engulfed by the avalanche.

The realisation of how close to death she had come wasn't something she could deal with right now.

She heard cracks and creaks as tree branches began to break under the weight of snow on them. And then a voice, harsh with urgency.

'*Holly!* Thank God!'

Jarek appeared from where the pine trees grew more densely and made his way over to where Holly was trapped against a tree trunk by the snow that had piled high around her like an icy straitjacket.

'I was afraid you'd been swept down the mountain,' he said unsteadily. 'But you're all right, angel-face, you're alive.'

He pulled a snow shovel from his backpack and started to dig away the snow around her.

'It's okay, baby. I'll get you out and back down the mountain in no time. You're safe. I'll take care of you.'

Despite being numb from shock, and the cold

that seemed to have turned the blood in her veins to ice, Holly was startled by the raw emotion in Jarek's voice. He brushed the snow away from her face and his blue eyes glittered with an odd intensity before he bent his head and claimed her mouth in a fierce kiss that stole what was left of her breath.

'I thought I'd lost you,' he muttered.

And then she knew she must be suffering from shock because he sounded as though it mattered— *she* mattered—to him.

It took several more minutes before he finally cleared the snow away from her legs and feet. 'Luckily you didn't lose your skis. Do you think you can ski the rest of the way down the mountain?'

'I'll have to. How else can we get down?'

Her numb sense of shock was fading, and feeling had returned to her body. She moved her arm and pain shot down from her shoulder all the way to her fingertips. The burning sensation was so agonising that she let out a scream.

'What's the matter?'

Jarek swore as her knees gave way and she almost blacked out. He caught her as her legs crumpled beneath her.

'Holly, are you hurt?'

'I've done something to my shoulder,' she told him through gritted teeth, trying desperately not to be sick.

The pain was so severe that she wondered how she could possibly ski when every slight movement was excruciating. She began to shiver uncontrollably, and was only partly aware of Jarek removing her skis.

When he took off his own skis, and fitted them into the carry-straps on his backpack, she stared at him. 'What are you doing?'

'There is an emergency shelter not far from here. We should be able to find it using the GPS on my phone. Once I've got you somewhere safe and warm I'll call the ski patrol and tell them you need to be airlifted off the mountain.'

'I'm sure that won't be necessary.' Holly hated making a fuss. 'I've probably just pulled a muscle in my shoulder and it will stop hurting soon—at least enough for me to ski down.'

She moved her arm gingerly and could not restrain a gasp of agony.

Jarek was studying a map on his phone's screen. 'The shelter is on the other side of the trees and over the next ridge. It should take approximately twenty minutes to walk to it from here.' He slipped his arm around her waist and leaned down to her. 'Put your arm round my neck.'

She shook her head when she realised his intention. 'You can't carry me. There's nothing wrong with my legs. I can walk.'

She took a step forward to prove her point, and discovered that the slightest movement made her shoulder hurt even more.

'Don't argue, Holly,' he said implacably. 'You're injured and shocked. The temperature will drop quickly, now that dusk is falling, and you're in danger of developing hypothermia.'

Holly didn't have the strength to disagree, and in truth she doubted she had the energy to walk any distance. She was colder than she had ever been in her life, and every shiver that juddered through her body sent a throb of searing pain to her shoulder.

Jarek carefully lifted her into his arms and she bit down hard on her lip to hold back a cry.

He carried her through the snow, and Holly was amazed by his strength and physical fitness. Several times she urged him to let her try to walk, but he refused. He did not even seem out of breath when they eventually arrived at a small wooden hut perched on a rocky outcrop and dwarfed by the towering Alps.

As soon as Jarek had opened the door and gently set her on her feet he pulled his phone out of his backpack. While he called the emergency services Holly looked around the hut. The furniture was basic—a narrow bed, a table and a couple of chairs—and at the far end of the hut was a small kitchen area with a wood-burner stove. She opened a door and found a toilet and a sink. At least the hut was safe and dry, but it felt no less cold inside than outside in the sub-zero temperature.

'It was lucky that we happened to ski fairly near to this emergency shelter,' she said to Jarek through her chattering teeth when he'd finished his phone call.

'Luck played no part in my decision of where to ski. Before we set out this morning I did some research and found out about this shelter—which is funded by donations and managed by the ski club in Arlenwald. I also checked the weather forecast and avalanche risk report—which was low. I certainly wouldn't have suggested skiing off-piste and putting our lives in danger if I'd thought there was any chance of an avalanche,' he said grimly.

He frowned as he watched her struggle to unfasten the chin-strap of her ski helmet while her body shook with uncontrollable shivers.

'Let me help you.' He came closer to help remove her helmet and swore softly. 'Your lips are turning blue—which is a sign you're developing hypothermia.'

'I think snow got into the top of my ski suit when I was caught in the avalanche. The lining of my jacket is wet,' Holly mumbled. She was finding it hard to talk coherently, and all she wanted to do was go to sleep.

Jarek moved over to the fireplace, where a pile of logs was stacked against the wall. 'I'm going to light a fire, and once the hut has warmed up I'll help you out of your ski gear. I brought some spare clothes in my pack, as well as emergency food supplies. We're going to have to spend the night in this hut,' he told her. 'The ski patrol can't get to us because they're dealing with a major incident further down the mountain. The avalanche swept away a group of skiers, and two people are still missing.'

Holly knew that if it had not been for Jarek's quick thinking she could have been swept away by the avalanche and buried beneath the snow too. She prayed the rescue services would find the missing skiers in time—but it was now dark, and the chances of locating the skiers alive would lessen with every minute they remained buried.

She felt she should offer to help build the fire, but she was so cold that she had lost all sensation in her fingers and toes and she felt sick from the throbbing pain in her shoulder. *Snap out of it*, she ordered herself when she felt an inexplicable urge to burst into tears. She guessed it was shock that had made her feel helpless and unable to do anything other than slump on a chair.

Within a few minutes Jarek had got a fire going, and the orange flames threw out a cheery glow in the dark hut. He lit the kerosene lamp that was on the table and light flickered over the hard angles of his face as he drew Holly to her feet and tugged the zip of her jacket down.

Pain ricocheted through her shoulder when he began to pull her jacket off. '*Ow!* I'll have to leave my jacket on. It hurts too much to take it off.'

'Your body won't warm up while you're wearing wet clothes,' he said firmly. 'Let's get this over with. And then I've got some painkillers in my pack that you can take.'

He tugged off her boots and socks, and before Holly could argue had pulled down her salopettes and helped her to step out of them. Next he unzipped the thermal fleece she wore beneath her jacket. Her base layer was a sports vest which had an inbuilt support bra, and that too was damp from the snow that had got into her jacket and seeped through the layers of clothes to her skin.

Jarek hooked his fingers into the waistband of her thermal leggings and tugged them over her hips and down her legs.

'I'll keep my top on,' Holly said quickly when he moved his hands to the hem of her vest. She felt self-conscious as it was, standing in front of him in her knickers. And the knowledge that she was not wearing a bra brought a flush to her cheeks that had nothing to do with the heat from the fire.

'It's wet, so it comes off.'

He ignored her attempt to slap his hands away and tugged her top up and over her head.

'I don't know why you are acting so shy,' he said when she crossed her arms over her bare breasts and tried to stifle the gasp of pain caused by sudden movement.

Holly reassured herself that her nipples were as hard as pebbles because she was *cold*, and not because of the hot gleam in Jarek's eyes.

'I saw your breasts when you came to my room last night, and very pretty they are, too,' he drawled. 'But you can put this on to protect your modesty.' He handed her a shirt that he had taken out of his backpack. 'Do you want me to help you put it on?'

'I want you to go to hell,' she told him, anger and embarrassment overriding the pain in her shoulder for a moment as she turned away from him and pulled the shirt on, before fastening the buttons over her breasts.

Jarek's shirt was much too big for her, and

came down to her mid-thighs, but although her body was mostly covered Holly was very aware that she was nearly naked beneath the shirt, and trapped in an isolated mountain shelter with the sexiest man on the planet.

His mocking grin infuriated her even more. 'Your temper is back so you must be feeling better, angel-face.'

'I wish you wouldn't call me that,' she snapped, hating the way her heart flipped when he pushed his hair back from his face, drawing her attention to the chiselled beauty of his hard features.

He was so tall that his head almost brushed against the roof of the hut, and his mane of thick blond hair and the darker blond stubble on his jaw added to Holly's impression of him as a Viking invader who was a dangerous threat to her heart.

'But it's true...' His tone was suddenly serious. 'You have the face of an angel.' He moved away to the far end of the hut and murmured, just loud enough for Holly to hear him, 'Not to mention a body that would tempt a saint.'

CHAPTER SEVEN

HOLLY JERKED HER eyes away from Jarek as he began to strip off his ski jacket and salopettes. She knelt in front of the fire, and when he joined her a few minutes later she silently cursed her accelerated heart-rate when she saw he had changed into a pair of sweatpants that sat low on his hips. She guessed he had only brought one spare shirt, which she was wearing. In the firelight the whorls of hair that covered his chest and arrowed down over his flat stomach were pure gold.

He dumped a pile of blankets on the floor. 'I found these in a storage box. We'll stay close to the fire and keep it burning through the night. You'll soon warm up,' he assured her, wrapping a blanket around her.'

He moved away to the kitchen and a short while later came back and handed her a steaming mug of hot chocolate.

Holly stared at him. 'How on earth...?'

'I brought packets of instant chocolate powder in my backpack, as well as bottled water which I boiled on the stove,' he explained. He gave her a foil blister-pack of pills. 'These are just non-prescription painkillers, but they might help dull the pain in your shoulder. As soon as we get off the mountain tomorrow you'll need to have it X-rayed.'

Jarek dropped down to sit on the floor beside her and put another log on the fire. They sipped their drinks in an oddly companionable silence. Holly felt relieved, and grateful to be safe after her terror in the avalanche. The overly sweet hot chocolate tasted better than anything she had ever drunk, and sitting in front of the fire, she was finally starting to feel warm again.

It was a novelty to have someone take care of her, she mused. She had moved away from her family when she was eighteen and she valued her independence—especially since Stuart had ended his relationship with her when she'd told him she could not give him a child. She'd had to accept that she might always be alone and had told herself she was fine with that. Today on the mountain she had felt more vulnerable than she had ever felt in her life, but she hadn't doubted that she could rely on Jarek to save her. Once again he had shown her a different side to him than the careless playboy image portrayed by the tabloids.

He had been her client for a week, but she was still no closer to working out who was the real Jarek, she though ruefully. She glanced at him and her heart gave a jolt when she found him watching her, with an unholy gleam in his bright blue eyes that evoked a different kind of heat deep inside her. The firelight danced over his naked torso, highlighting his taut abdominal muscles and gilding his broad shoulders.

Their eyes met...held...and the atmosphere inside the hut altered subtly from cosy to something far more dangerous.

Holly heard herself swallow and quickly looked away from him. 'You make a good fire,' she murmured, searching for something to say. 'Were you a boy scout? I can't imagine where else you would have learned your impressive survival skills.'

'No, I don't suppose you, or anyone who has not lived through a war, can imagine what it's like to hear the constant noise of mortar fire and wonder if the next bombardment will strike what is left of the building you're sheltering in,' he said, somewhat drily.

She bit her lip. 'That was thoughtless of me. Of course you weren't a boy scout. You didn't have a chance to enjoy normal childhood activities growing up in Sarajevo.'

Jarek raked his hand through his hair and stared at the flames leaping around the logs. 'I was taught how to build a fire by the soldiers who were defending the city. I got friendly with some of them, and I would run messages along the frontline because I was small enough to avoid being noticed by the attacking troops.' He shrugged. 'The enemy snipers took no notice of a half-starved nine-year-old boy. When the orphanage was bombed I used whatever I could find—chair legs and bits of broken door—to make a fire to keep the younger children warm. My survival skills were learned out of necessity.'

'I'm sorry I said I wanted you to go to hell,' Holly said in a low tone. 'You spent your childhood there, didn't you?'

She pictured Jarek as a young boy, struggling

to survive and take care of his baby sister and the other orphaned children who had been innocent victims of a brutal war.

'I haven't thanked you for saving my life,' she whispered. 'I dread to think what would have happened to me if I had been on my own when the avalanche struck.'

She flinched when he swore.

'You wouldn't have been on that part of the mountain if it wasn't for my bloody irresponsible decision to take you skiing off-piste,' he said savagely. 'It is entirely my fault that you are hurt and having to spend the night in an emergency shelter.'

'It was my *choice* to ski off-piste,' Holly insisted. 'Far from being irresponsible, you knew the location of the hut before we set out and you were well prepared for an emergency.'

He gave a bitter laugh. 'Don't try and make me out as a hero. Ralph was right when he accused me of having a destructive streak. I ruin lives and I destroy everything that is good—including Lorna.' His voice dropped to a raw growl, as if he was in pain. 'Especially Mama...'

'Who is Ralph?' Holly asked quietly.

'Ralph Saunderson was my adoptive father. He and his wife Lorna rescued my sister and me from the orphanage in Sarajevo.' He grimaced. 'I don't think Ralph particularly enjoyed fatherhood. He didn't care for his own son, much less me—a feral boy with a chip on his shoulder and an aversion to authority. But Lorna was a wonderful mother to Elin and me. It broke my sister's heart when Mama died.'

Jarek dropped his head into his hands.

'It was my fault. I was responsible for my adoptive mother's death as much as if I had fired the shot that killed her. I didn't need that bloody journalist to point out the fact to me,' he muttered.'

Holly frowned. 'Are you referring to the journalist you assaulted at a press conference, after you were involved in that crash during a motorbike race?'

'The journalist accused me of riding recklessly and endangering the safety of the other competitors in the race—which wasn't true...the race stewards had no concerns about how I'd ridden. But the press love to stir up trouble, and that journalist dug up the story from four years ago about Lorna's death. I lost my temper because I couldn't bear to be reminded of what I'd done,' he admitted heavily.

'What did you do?' she asked softly.

She wanted to reach out and put her hand on Jarek's hunched shoulders, somehow magic away the pain that she had heard in his voice. He seemed so alone, and with a flash of insight she realised that his party-loving playboy image in the press was a façade he used to hide his tormented soul.

He gave a heavy sigh, as if he was worn down by the burden he had carried for so long. 'It was Mama's birthday, and Elin and I had taken her to a jeweller's so that she could choose a gift.' His voice was a harsh scrape of sound. 'We were the only customers in the shop when a man walked in and pulled out a pistol. He ordered me, my sister and the shop assistant to lie down on the floor, and he aimed the gun at Lorna while he grabbed jewellery from the display cases.'

Jarek's jaw clenched.

'I could tell the guy was nervous. When he dragged Lorna towards the door I guessed he intended to take her with him as a hostage. She was terrified, and crying, and the gunman was shouting at her to shut up. In the confusion I seized my chance and managed to rugby tackle him to the floor. But before I could grab the gun he pulled the trigger. The bullet went straight through Mama's heart, killing her instantly.'

'Jarek, it wasn't your fault.'

Holly's heart splintered when she saw a tear slip down his cheek. The firelight flickered over the angles and planes of his face, where the skin was stretched taut and his mouth was so grim that it was hard to imagine his trademark sexy grin. He never smiled with his eyes, she realised.

He did not seem to have heard her. 'My recklessness killed her,' he rasped, as if he had swallowed glass. 'The soldiers in Sarajevo had a motto: *Shoot first or be shot*. But I didn't have a gun, and my decision to tackle an armed robber was crassly irresponsible.'

'I believe you acted instinctively to protect your adoptive mother.' she said gently. 'As a young boy you had protected your sister from the dangers of war. Childhood experiences frequently affect our behaviour as adults, and your determination to take care of people in need of help was programmed into you when you were nine years old.'

He turned his head towards her and she wanted to weep when she saw the torment that dulled his blue eyes, and the flash of vulnerability that flickered on his face before he let his hair fall forward to hide his expression.

'Lorna died as a result of an unforgivable act, but *you* did not fire the gun that ended her life and *you* were in no way to blame,' Holly told him fiercely.

She reached out and placed her hand on his forearm, hoping the physical contact would in some small way ease the loneliness that she sensed never left him. She guessed that this was the first time he had ever spoken about his guilty feelings over his adoptive mother's death.

'The only life you are careless with is your own. You must have known that the armed man who robbed the jewellery shop could have aimed his gun at you, but that didn't stop you trying your best to protect Lorna.' She bit her lip. 'I wish you could see what I see. You are a brave and good man, Jarek.'

'If that is really what you see then I suggest you

need your eyesight tested,' he said mockingly, but there was a note almost of desperation in his voice as he picked up her hand and threaded his fingers through hers.

Holly sensed that he wanted to believe her, but he couldn't allow himself to do so because he was convinced there could be no redemption for him.

'I wish I had followed my instincts when I arrived at the Frieden Clinic. You knocked me senseless with your beautiful smile, before announcing that you were my psychotherapist and we would be living together for six weeks,' he said harshly. 'For your safety and my sanity I should have jumped back onto my motorbike and ridden far away from you.'

'I'm glad you didn't,' she whispered.

In a distant corner of her mind Holly was aware that the painkillers had done their job, and when she moved she felt only a twinge instead of the agonising sensation of a red-hot poker being thrust into her shoulder.

She assured herself that all she wanted to do was offer Jarek comfort as she knelt in front of him and placed her hands on either side of his face. But even that small contact between their bodies created an electrical current that shot through her, and she could not restrain a soft gasp as heat unfurled low in her belly.

His bright blue eyes glittered as hard as diamonds. 'You're playing with fire, angel-face,' he said, in an oddly thick voice. 'You would be safer outside on the mountain than in here with me. There are things you don't know about me. Secrets I don't even know about myself.'

His beautiful mouth twisted.

'A long time ago I think I did something so terrible that my mind has blocked out my memories. You told me that *is* possible,' he growled, when she traced her fingertips over the rough stubble on his jaw. 'For all either of us know I could be a monster... I don't know...a murderer.' He glared at her when she didn't cower away from him. 'I don't know *what* I am,' he said grimly, 'but I do know that I'm no good for you.'

It occurred to Holly then that Jarek was trying to protect her from himself, as if he really *did* believe he was a monster, and her heart ached for him.

'I do think something bad happened to you when you were a child, but I don't believe for one second that you are a bad person. Besides,' she murmured in a deliberately lighter voice, 'I'm not suggesting that we align our diaries for the next few months.'

His eyes narrowed when she quoted the exact same words he had said to her after that explosive kiss in his bedroom at Chalet Soline. She sensed that some of his fierce tension had left him, and his mouth crooked in a lazy smile that made her tremble almost as much as the feral gleam in his eyes.

'What are you suggesting, then?' he drawled, all arrogant male confidence once more.

On one level Holly wondered what on earth she was doing. Perhaps her close brush with death on the mountain was the reason for the wildness that filled her, and made her wonder how she had resisted him until now.

'This,' she whispered against his lips, before she covered his mouth with hers.

He went very still, and her stomach plummeted when she thought he was going to push her away. But then he made a noise in his throat—a low growl of hunger that connected directly to the molten core of her femininity. His arms closed around her like steel bars and he sank his fingers into her hair at the same time as he thrust his tongue into her mouth and took command of a kiss that quickly became a ravishment of her senses.

He should bring an end to this right now, Jarek told himself. Before the feel of Holly's lips pressed against his became an addiction he would never be able to break. But the sweet ardency of her kiss and—dear God—her *generosity* evoked something inside him that he had never felt with any other woman. *'I don't believe you are a bad person,'* she had said, in stark contrast to everyone else throughout his life, who had said the opposite. Not his sister, of course, but Elin's loyalty made her blind to his faults. Even Mama had been fond of him *despite* his flaws, as if he was a challenge or a penance.

No one apart from Holly had ever suggested that he might be any good. But unfortunately she was wrong. If there was any shred of goodness in him then he would *not* tumble her down onto the pile of blankets in front of the fire and stretch out beside her. He would *not* cradle her jaw in his palm and kiss her with unrestrained hunger. And he would *not* take such delight in her soft sigh of surrender when he unbuttoned the shirt he had lent her and played with her breasts.

Her nipples puckered in anticipation of his touch, and she gave a thin cry when he traced moist circles around one aureole with his tongue before drawing the hard nub at its centre into his mouth and sucking—hard. The greedy sounds she made became ever more frantic when he transferred his mouth to her other breast, and because he was bad he took fierce pleasure in the way her hips jerked off the floor in an invitation he had no intention of declining.

The firelight flickered over her body and Jarek followed the path of the flames with his tongue to explore every delicious dip and curve…the smooth slopes of her breasts, the indentation of her waist, and down, down to taste the silken skin of her inner thighs. He laughed softly at the muffled sound she made—half-protest, half-plea—when he hooked his fingers into her panties and tugged them down her legs.

She was so sweetly responsive that it made him ache deep in his gut. And he was so hard.

Sweet heaven, he was more turned on than he could ever remember being. He wanted to pull her beneath him and sink between her milky-white thighs, drive his rock-solid shaft into her slick heat and glory in the fiery passion that had simmered between them for what seemed like an eternity, but in fact was only one week. Six weeks with this woman would kill him, Jarek thought wryly. Worse still, he might be tempted to tell Holly what he saw in his nightmares, and then she would know for sure that there was nothing good about him.

But he would not have months or weeks or even any more days with her. She could not save him, however much she believed that therapy would help him. Jarek knew he must walk away from her before he destroyed her, as he had almost done today on the mountain, and just as he had destroyed Mama. There was only this one night, and he was arrogant enough to want her, even as mindless with desire as he was.

But this wasn't about him. Tonight was all about Holly.

He felt a tremor run through her when he dipped his tongue into her navel and then pressed soft kisses over her stomach. But when he pushed her legs apart and knelt between her thighs she stiffened.

'You can't...'

Her shocked whisper was barely audible, and he grinned at her before he bent his head.

'Oh, yes, I can, angel-face,' he assured her thickly.

His nostrils flared as he caught the sweet scent of her arousal and he could not wait any longer. He slid his hands beneath her bottom and lifted her towards him, holding her at just the right angle. He had never seen a more beautiful sight than her splayed open before him. With a growl of satisfaction he set about his appointed task, and with his tongue bestowed the most intimate caress of all.

She made a startled sound, as if what he was doing to her was new, and her fingers gripped his hair. When he placed his mouth over the tight little nub of her clitoris she gave a sharp cry as she shattered around him.

Jarek didn't know how he found the strength of will to ignore the thunderous drumbeat of his own desire—especially when Holly tried to slide her hand beneath the waistband of his sweatpants. But she had been shocked and scared in the aftermath of the avalanche, and he knew that if he took advantage of her vulnerability he would hate himself even more than he already did.

He hadn't finished with her yet, though, and while she was still panting and gasping from her first orgasm he pressed his mouth against her riotous heat once more and took possession of her with a mastery that had her sobbing his name as she climaxed again.

Afterwards he drew her trembling body against him and held her against his chest—against the heart that ached dully as she fell asleep in his arms and he watched over her for the rest of the night to keep her safe.

The cold woke her. Holly opened her eyes and felt disorientated for a few seconds, before she remembered that she had spent the night in an emergency shelter halfway up a mountain. A shaft of bright light came into the hut through the one small window, and she registered that the fire had gone out and there was no sign of Jarek.

Memories rushed into her mind, followed swiftly by self-recrimination.

What had she done?

More pertinently, what had she allowed *Jarek* to do?

She turned her head slowly, expecting to see him at the far end of the hut. The sight of her knickers on the floor next to her was a reminder of just how bad the situation was, but in case she was in any doubt images flashed into her head of her sprawled on the floor, with her legs wide apart and Jarek on his knees, holding her thighs firmly open with his hands as he leaned forward and put his mouth *there*, right at her feminine core.

Worse than the erotic images in her mind was the accompanying soundtrack: her pants and gasps culminating in the keening cry that had been torn from her when he'd made her come— *twice*. And his laughter…deep and husky…the memory of it even now brought her skin out in goosebumps that had nothing to do with the bitterly cold temperature inside the hut.

She briefly debated if it would have been preferable to have been swept to her doom by the avalanche than to be lying here facing humiliation and dismissal from her job. The knowledge that her behaviour had been unprofessional, to say the least, prompted her to get up from the floor— but she quickly discovered that the effects of the painkillers had worn off and a sickening bolt of pain throbbed in her shoulder.

It was imperative for what remained of her dignity that she put her knickers back on before she faced Jarek and so, gritting her teeth, she forced herself to bend down and pick them up. She had just managed to pull them on and struggle into her salopettes when the door of the hut opened and he walked in.

'Good—you're awake,' he said coolly, with no hint in his voice of the sensual lover from the previous night.

Holly's fragile hope that he would sweep her into his arms withered and died. He was dressed in his ski clothes and his eyes were hidden behind designer shades. With his just-got-out-of-bed blond hair falling over his collar he looked like one of the beautiful people who flocked to St Moritz or Klosters.

A sense of hopelessness swept over Holly as

she acknowledged that she was not a glamorous socialite or an A-list female celebrity, like the women Jarek was used to. His cavalier attitude this morning made her think he had made love to her simply because they had been stranded on the mountain and he'd probably been bored.

But their enforced proximity had not been the only reason, a nasty little voice in her head taunted her. She had thrown herself at him with all the finesse of a gauche teenager. It was likely that he had kissed her out of politeness, because he hadn't wanted to embarrass her by rejecting her clumsy overtures. If he had really desired her then surely he would have wanted to have full-blown sex with her?

Thank heaven he hadn't tried to, she thought, going hot and then cold as she imagined how humiliating it would have been if she'd had to explain that she was different from other women. Flawed.

'The helicopter is on its way.'

His brisk voice jerked her from her painful thoughts.

'Can you manage to put your jacket on if I help you?'

She remembered how tenderly he had taken care of her when he had carried her to the shelter. Clearly she had misconstrued his attentiveness and taken it as a sign that he felt something for her.

'I think you've done enough,' she said curtly, glad of the hot flare of temper to replace the mortification that bit deep into her soul.

'I didn't hear you object last night,' he drawled, and his softly mocking tone made her long to sink through the floor.

She wished she could see the expression in his eyes, which were hidden behind his sunglasses. She felt exposed and, worse, she felt foolish for wanting him to claim her mouth with his and brand her with the hungry passion that had devoured them both—or so she had believed.

She had made a fool of herself, Holly thought miserably.

The *whump, whump* of a helicopter's rotor blades was a welcome distraction. Jarek moved towards her and seemed about to say something, but just then a paramedic walked into the hut and started questioning Holly about the injury she had received. While she explained about the pain in her shoulder, and then insisted that she could walk and did not need to be carried on a stretcher, Jarek stepped outside.

The paramedic wrapped a foil blanket around her to raise her body temperature and helped her walk across the snow to the waiting helicopter. It was only when she was strapped into a seat and the helicopter was about to take off that she panicked, realising Jarek was not on board.

'Your friend decided to ski down the mountain,' the paramedic explained. We'll fly you straight to the hospital. Try not to worry—you are safe now.'

Holly wasn't worried for herself, but she *was* concerned about Jarek. Last night had been the first time he had opened up to her and revealed his guilt over his adoptive mother's death. She was convinced he would find counselling beneficial, but *she* could no longer be his psychotherapist. Not after she had behaved like a slut and allowed him to take shocking liberties with her body.

She winced as she pictured herself naked in front of the fire, her principles abandoned and her legs spread wide. Her sense of honour demanded she must tell Professor Heppel that she could not continue in her role as Jarek's counsellor because of a conflict of interest.

Several hours later a hospital doctor studied an X-ray of Holly's shoulder and confirmed that it wasn't broken, merely sprained and badly bruised from the impact of the avalanche. She was given strong painkillers and advised to rest her shoulder as much as possible for the next few days.

She knew she had escaped lightly, and Professor Heppel expressed the same opinion after Gunther had collected her from the hospital and driven her to Chalet Soline.

Holly had expected Jarek to be at the chalet, and her heart sank when Professor Heppel told her that he had checked out of the Frieden Clinic.

'Obviously I will resign immediately,' she said stiffly, thinking it would be marginally less embarrassing to leave of her own accord than to be fired for professional misconduct.

The clinic's director looked puzzled. 'Why do you wish to resign? Mr Dvorska gave an excellent report on how you had helped him in the brief time he was here. He has cut short his stay at the clinic because he heard this morning that his sister has given birth to her baby—several weeks early. I understand that there were complications with the birth and Jarek has gone to England to be with his sister.'

Holly's relief that Jarek had not made a complaint about her inappropriate conduct was short-lived as she prayed that Elin and her baby were both all right. His concern for his sister might explain why he had been so off-hand with her at the hut, she brooded. He would have been impatient to get off the mountain, and understandably his thoughts would have been focused on Elin.

For the next few days she was virtually housebound, while her injured shoulder gradually healed, and with time on her hands she found her thoughts centred on Jarek, and the notion that he had been distracted by worry for his sister rather than deliberately dismissive of the scorching passion they had shared. When she had knelt in front of him and kissed him he might have rejected her. But he had kissed her with a fierce intensity, as if he had been lost in a desert and had suddenly stumbled on an oasis where he could assuage his thirst.

The idea that he had responded to her out of a gentlemanly desire to save her from embarrassment just didn't fit. She was thirty-one, and although she did not have a long list of previous lovers she was experienced enough to recognise white-hot lust. Jarek's erection had been as hard as a spike beneath his sweatpants, so he couldn't have been pretending to desire her. It had been the real thing.

His mobile phone number was in his file. Holly reminded herself that it was not unusual for a therapist to call an ex-patient for a follow-up report after they had left the clinic, but her hands shook as she entered his number on her phone.

He answered on the third ring, and his sexy, smoky voice curled around her like a caress. She grimaced when she felt her nipples tighten. If he could have such a strong effect on her when he was a thousand miles away, God help her if he asked to see her again.

'Hi, Jarek, it's me…um…' She flushed, 'I mean Dr Maitland…from the Frieden Clinic.'

'I'm perfectly aware of who you are, Holly,' he drawled, sounding amused, and she just *knew* that he knew that her face was scarlet.

She cleared her throat. 'I called to ask how your sister and her baby are. I mean… I hope they are okay.'

She sensed his surprise and wished she'd listened to her common sense, which had urged her not to phone him.

'Mother and baby are both fine now. Elin had a health scare in the late stages of her pregnancy and her daughter had to be delivered by Caesarean section a month early. Rosalie is tiny but healthy, my sister is over the moon and my brother-in-law is besotted with the two females in his life,' Jarek said drily.

'I'm glad.' She hesitated. 'I want to apologise for snapping at you in the morning…after we had spent the night in the emergency shelter. I thought you regretted what had happened between us. But then I heard from Professor Heppel that you had rushed away to be with your sister.'

Jarek's silence on the other end of the line wasn't encouraging, but Holly ploughed on.

'I was hoping to persuade you to continue your course of treatment with another psychotherapist. Clearly I cannot be your therapist due to our personal relationship—'

'I hardly think that one night together consti-
tutes a *relationship*,' he interrupted curtly. 'I told
you—I don't have relationships. What happened
between us in the hut was a mistake brought
about by an excess of adrenalin after we had
survived the avalanche.'

Ow!

Holly gripped her phone tighter and told herself
to end the call now—this second. But she must
have a masochistic streak, because she muttered,
'An excess of adrenalin? Really? Most people
would call what we both felt...*feel*...desire.'

'Look, Holly—' he sounded impatient '—we
had a good time together but it wasn't memo-
rable—at least not for me. I suggest you forget
me. You're a nice girl, and you deserve to meet
a great guy who will fall in love with you.'

This was worse than *ow*! It was excruciatingly
embarrassing. Holly wanted to die a thousand
deaths, but pride forced her to say lightly, 'I'm
thirty-one. By no stretch of the imagination could
I be described as a "girl". I'm sorry I made the
mistake of believing that beneath your playboy
image there was a man of substance.' And then,
because she was innately truthful, she said qui-

etly, 'As a matter of fact I *still* believe you are a better man than you think, and I urge you to engage a counsellor to help you face up to your past.'

She ended the call before he could say anything else she did not want to hear. The knowledge that her humiliation was self-induced, because against her better judgement she had phoned him, only made her feel worse. She wanted to burst into tears. Instead she gave in to the childish urge to throw her phone across the room and heard a satisfying thud as it hit the wall.

CHAPTER EIGHT

JAREK CRADLED HIS phone in his hand long after it had gone silent, as if holding it would somehow prolong his contact with Holly. He knew he would not hear from her again—which had been his intention when he'd rejected her so cruelly. Right from the start he had wanted to protect her from his destructive nature, but he'd been able to tell from the huskiness in her voice that he had hurt her—and not only her pride.

Yet despite her obvious embarrassment she had told him she still believed in him, thought that he was a better man than he knew himself to be. He wished it was true, but he was afraid that the dark shadows in his mind hid even darker secrets.

It was why he had left Austria and flown to London immediately after he'd skied down the mountain where he had so nearly been responsible for another tragic death. He went cold when he thought of how easily Holly could have been swept away by the avalanche. He'd checked out of the Frieden Clinic because he did not want her to discover that her faith in him had been misplaced.

He turned away from the window and the uninspiring view of a bleak winter sky and the bare skeletons of the trees. February in England was his least favourite time of the year. In another month or two the Cuckmere Hall estate on the South Downs would begin to look green, rather than grey and dead, and Elin would no longer be fretting about frost damaging the new shoots in the estate's vineyards.

Although at the moment his sister was too enamoured of her brand-new baby daughter to have time to worry about Saunderson's Wines, Jarek mused.

He had never shared Elin's interest in the winery that Lorna Saunderson had established. But Elin's husband Cortez was a world-renowned vintner, and the sparkling wine now produced on the estate had won several prestigious awards.

Jarek looked across the room to where his sister and brother-in-law were sitting close together on the sofa. Elin was cradling baby Rosalie and Cortez was bouncing their two-year-old son Harry on his knee. They were the perfect family, and Jarek certainly did not begrudge them their obvious happiness. Despite a rocky start he and Cortez had become friends, and he was always made to feel welcome at Cuckmere Hall. But he had never felt that he belonged at the gothic mansion he had once expected to inherit from Ralph Saunderson. And anyway Ralph had chosen his illegitimate son to be his heir, rather than the adopted son he had accused of being reckless.

Moodily, Jarek walked over to the fireplace, where a cheery fire burned in the grate. Under Cortez's supervision Cuckmere Hall had been transformed from a draughty old house to a stylish and comfortable home. But it wasn't Jarek's home any more than his starkly minimalist penthouse in London or the various other properties he owned around the world felt like home.

An image flashed into his mind of a big, bright room. Sunlight streamed in through the windows and there was a wooden rocking horse—white, with a red harness. He heard a child laughing, and with a jolt of shock he realised that the child was *him*. He couldn't have been at the orphanage, he realised, because he did not remember ever laughing there. He sensed that the room he could visualise was a nursery, and knew without knowing *how* he knew that he had felt safe there, and—his heart gave a lurch—*loved*. Was the vague figure in his mind whose face he could not quite see his *mother*?

'I saw Baines carrying your suitcase downstairs.'

Elin's voice jerked him back to the present, and to his bitter frustration the images in his head disappeared like smoke drifting up the chimney.

'Are you going back to the clinic in Austria?'

'No.' He felt a stab of guilt at his sister's concerned expression.

'How did you get on with Dr Maitland? She sounded nice when I spoke to her.' Elin gave him a close look. Is she pretty?' she asked mischievously.

He pictured Holly lying in front of the fire, with her silky brown hair spread around her shoulders and her naked body so unutterably beautiful that he had sunk to his knees and worshipped her.

'Pretty enough, I suppose,' he said dismissively.

'But I prefer fun-loving blondes to serious brunettes.'

Or that had been true in the past—before he had met his beautiful psychotherapist, he brooded.

'I'm going to Vostov,' he said abruptly, steering the conversation away from Holly.

'The principality has been in the news recently,' Cortez commented. 'Rumours abound that the ruling family of the House of Karadjvic may have been murdered during the conflict in the Balkans in the early nineteen-nineties. And there is another rumour that the royal children might have survived.'

'But those children would be adults now—surely they'd know if they were royalty,' Elin said.

Cortez shrugged. 'Perhaps they were too young at the time for them to remember.' He glanced at Jarek. 'Are you thinking of investing in Vostov? The low business taxes there have enabled the principality to establish a thriving economy.'

'I've arranged to meet someone to discuss various things,' Jarek said noncommittally.

If he told Elin of his crazy suspicion that their parents had been a prince and princess she would insist that he sought help from a psychiatrist. He could not tell anyone the real reason for his trip to Vostov was so that he could meet Asmir Sunjic.

Jarek was certain the old man's story was an elaborate hoax. But his nightmares were becoming more frequent and troubling, and he was determined to find out the truth about his past.

Twenty-four hours later Jarek rode the motorbike he had hired along a twisting mountain road in Vostov, on his way to a remote village. The landscape of tall pine trees and snow-capped mountains was similar to Alpine countries, which might explain why it seemed familiar. Harder to explain was the sense of belonging he'd felt the moment his private jet had landed at a small airfield. He had not wanted to draw attention to his visit by arriving at the principality's main airport.

He was sure he recognised the style of the traditional grey stone houses with steeply sloping tin roofs as he rode into the village. Some of the villagers came out to stare at him as he knocked on the door of a house. An elderly woman ushered him inside. She spoke in a language that sounded similar to Bosnian and Jarek guessed was Vostovian. He was startled to find that he understood some of the woman's words, but then his attention swung to the old man who slowly rose out of a chair next to the fire.

Time had left its mark on the man's features, but Jarek knew he had seen him before—a long time ago—and pain ripped through him as if he had been shot through his heart.

From the air, the tiny island of Paradis sur Terre looked like an emerald jewel set amid a cerulean sea. As the helicopter descended Holly saw that most of the island was covered in dense green forest and surrounded by pure white sandy beaches. Even the name which, translated from the French, meant Heaven on Earth, was a perfect description of the privately owned island in the Indian Ocean.

It was a pity there was a serpent in paradise.

Her stomach muscles tightened as the helicopter swooped low over the one building on the island—a charming colonial-style house with direct access onto the beach. A wooden jetty ran from the beach out over the crystal-clear sea, and at the far end of the jetty stood a blond-haired Viking.

Holly's heart gave a jolt when she caught sight of Jarek, and she almost asked the pilot to fly her back to the international airport in the Seychelles capital city of Victoria. She must have been mad to agree to his request to see him again, let alone fly halfway round the world to meet him, she thought for the hundredth time. Although Jarek had not so much requested as *demanded* that she be on the private jet he had sent to Austria to bring her to the Seychelles.

Her mind flew back forty-eight hours, to when she'd answered her phone without first glancing at the screen to check the name of the caller. The sound of Jarek's voice had nearly made her drop her phone which was still held together with tape after their last conversation three weeks ago had resulted in her hurling the handset at the wall.

'I've decided to take your advice and carry on with therapy,' Jarek had told her, ignoring any conventional greeting like *Hello, how are you?* Although even if he had asked she would have rather died than admit that she felt sick with misery and had lost her enthusiasm for life since he had left Austria.

'I think your decision is sensible.' She had been pleased that she sounded cool and calm when her heart had been pounding. 'All the clinical staff here at the Frieden Clinic are highly qualified to help you. I'll check with Professor Heppel to see which of them is available to give you counselling.'

'I don't want a different psychotherapist. I want you.'

Jarek's smoky voice had wreaked havoc with Holly's equilibrium. Just when she had been making progress in forgetting him, she'd thought, but had known she was fooling herself.

'I'm afraid that's not possible. My schedule is full and I will be working with other patients,' she'd told him crisply.

'Your other patients might change their mind and decide not to seek treatment from you if they hear about how you behaved so unprofessionally with me. Social media is *very* useful for spreading rumours,' he'd drawled. 'And when Professor Heppel reads my report concerning certain aspects of my experience as a patient at his clinic—

which I will email to him if you refuse to see me—you may even find yourself out of a job.'

She'd felt sick 'You wouldn't do that.'

'I told you—I don't play fair, angel-face.'

'As a matter of fact, blackmail is illegal,' she'd said tersely.

'I admit I might have embellished a few details about the night we spent together in that mountain hut...'

Beneath his amused tone Holly had heard quiet determination and had felt her heart sink.

'Jarek...you must see that I can't be your psychotherapist,' she'd argued desperately. 'It wouldn't be right—'

'You are the only person I trust,' he had interrupted her harshly. And then, even more shockingly, 'I need you, Holly. I have to talk to you.'

Fool that she was, she had felt her heart melt at the rawness in his voice. The outrageous attempt to coerce her into agreeing to visit him on his remote island hideaway had struck her as strange behaviour from the feckless playboy he was portrayed as being in the tabloids. But Holly knew that behind his public image Jarek had integrity and compassion. He'd said he trusted her, and she could not allow her pride to prevent her from helping him deal with his demons.

The helicopter landed on a green lawn in front of the house, and Holly was greeted by a cheerful man in a white uniform who introduced himself as the butler, Rani.

'I'll take your case up to the house, Dr Maitland. Mr Dvorska is waiting for you on the beach,' Rani told her.

She soon discovered that walking on soft sand in kitten-heel shoes was no easy task. The late-afternoon sun was blazing in a cloudless azure sky, and by the time she stepped onto the jetty Holly felt hot and was tempted to take off her jacket. But she could not risk her body betraying her as she walked towards Jarek. Her grey wool suit and crisp white blouse were her armour against his potency.

He must have heard her heels tapping on the wooden boards because he turned around. Holly's footsteps faltered. She had thought about him constantly in the past weeks, but he was even more breathtaking than her memories of him.

He was wearing a pair of faded denim shorts that sat low on his hips. His chest was bare and his dark golden tan suggested that he had spent much of the past three weeks in the sun. Holly's eyes roamed over his flat stomach and the defined ridges of his impressive six-pack. Lifting her gaze higher to his face, she noted there was at least three days' growth of stubble on his jaw, and the too-long hair that he was pushing off his brow had been bleached even blonder by the sun.

His wide mouth crooked in a sexy smile, but his ice-blue eyes were as hard as diamonds and revealed nothing of his thoughts.

'Hello, Holly,' he murmured, in the gravelly voice that she had heard countless times in her dreams.

She felt a rush of heat to her breasts, and was conscious of the tendrils of sweat-damp hair that clung to her flushed cheeks. 'It's so hot!' she burst out, desperate to fill the awkward silence and disguise the thunderous beat of her heart. 'The temperature was minus two when I left Austria.'

'Is that why you are dressed for arctic conditions?' he said drily. 'The daytime temperature in the Seychelles at this time of year rarely drops below thirty degrees, and the dress code is informal. Wear as little as you like.' His wicked grin made her catch her breath. 'I hope you packed your gold swimsuit.'

'Stop right there,' Holly told him firmly. She held up her hand, as if she could ward off his charisma. 'I know that flirting is as natural to you as breathing, but you don't have to switch on your fake charm with me because you've already established that I'm nice but unmemorable.'

Something flashed in his eyes. 'I'm sorry I hurt you,' he said roughly.

He stepped closer to her and she immediately backed away from him.

'I'm old enough to cope with rejection gracefully, and I'm sure I'll survive having my ego dented.' She shrugged. 'I was simply under the misapprehension that you liked me.'

'Of course I bloody well *like* you.' He took another step towards her and caught hold of her arm. 'The night we spent together in that mountain hut was amazing. It was—'

'It was a mistake,' Holly insisted. She looked at him steadily. ' I'm prepared to try to help you, but I won't be fobbed off with excuses or chase you around the island like I chased you up that mountain. You say you want to talk to me—so talk.'

He stared at her, clearly surprised by her refusal to be a push-over, and there was reluctant admiration in his voice when he spoke. 'You've had a long journey to get here. Come up to the house and I'll show you to your room. I'm sure you want to change into something cooler,' he said, eyeing her thick skirt and jacket. 'I guessed you wouldn't have had a chance to buy beachwear in Austria, so I took the liberty of buying a few summer clothes for you.'

He started to walk back along the jetty and Holly had no choice but to follow him.

'I've asked the chef to prepare an early dinner,' he said over his shoulder. 'We'll talk then.'

Twenty minutes later Holly felt refreshed after taking a shower. Her bedroom was delightfully cool, thanks to the ceiling fan that was positioned over the huge bed. Sliding glass doors opened onto a balcony where pots of white jasmine grew in profusion, filling the room with their delicate fragrance. From the balcony she could see a turquoise infinity pool that looked tempting—

although she had definitely *not* packed the frivolous gold swimsuit Jarek had referred to.

What would he think of her sensible blue costume? she wondered, and then reminded herself that she didn't care about his opinion of her.

She rifled through her clothes, which the maid had unpacked and hung in the wardrobe, and realised she would swelter if she wore any of the smart business suits she had brought to the island with her.

Hanging on the rail next to her own clothes were the summer outfits that Jarek had provided: pretty dresses in lightweight fabrics that would be far more comfortable to wear in the heat. She would insist on paying for the clothes, Holly assured herself as she slipped on an elegant wraparound dress of aquamarine silk. Luckily she had packed a pair of flat ballet pumps that looked fine with the dress.

She had just caught her hair up in a loose knot on top of her head when the maid came to escort her to lunch.

Jarek was waiting for her beneath a gazebo next to the pool, where the butler was laying out a buffet-style meal on the table. Everything was so vivid, Holly thought, looking at the bowls of colourful salads and an array of fresh fruits. Bright pink hibiscus flowers covered the wooden frame of the gazebo, and the early-evening sunshine dappled everything in a mellow golden light.

'This is an incredible place,' she said as she sat down and picked up the glass of sparkling water that Rani had served her. She was curious to see that Jarek had opted for fruit juice rather than wine.

'I haven't drunk alcohol or smoked a cigarette for weeks,' he told her. 'Sex is the only vice left,' he said, and grinned when she blushed.

Holly silently cursed her fair skin. 'I don't suppose you've given up *that* particular vice— even though there has been a notable absence of scandalous stories about your love-life in the tabloids recently. Perhaps you have decided to conduct your affairs with more discretion,' she said sweetly.

His smile faded and he seemed suddenly tense. 'I've been here on the island—alone apart from the staff. I flew here straight after I'd visited my sister and my new niece. Paradis sur Terre belongs to a friend of mine, and only he and you know my whereabouts.'

'Why the secrecy?' Holly frowned.

Jarek handed her a letter.

'Read it,' he urged her grimly.

Jarek was tempted to add a shot of rum to his pineapple juice. He had kept away from vodka since he'd left Austria, because every time he'd thought about having a drink he'd had the crazy idea that Holly would be disappointed with him. As if he *cared* about her opinion of him, he brooded. Right now he wanted to drink enough alcohol to render him unconscious, but he sipped his fruit juice and waited for Holly to finish reading Asmir Sunjic's astonishing letter.

He watched the sunlight slanting through the blinds on the gazebo spill over her hair, so that it gleamed in myriad shades from dark chocolate through to russet. Oddly, he felt calmer than he'd done in days—weeks. Three weeks, to be exact. Since he had checked out of the Frieden Clinic believing he would never see Holly again.

Now she was here in front of him, looking even more beautiful than he remembered. How he was managing to hold himself back from walking around the table and snatching her into his arms so that he could claim her mouth with his, as he had done a thousand times in his dreams, was beyond him.

She put the letter down on the table and stared at him, shock and disbelief in her dark eyes.

'I'm guessing from the stilted wording that English isn't this man Asmir Sunjic's first language, but the letter is clear enough. Is it some sort of joke? There can't be any truth in what he says, can there?' She shook her head. 'His story seems so fantastical.'

'That's what I thought at first, but now I don't know. Maybe his crazy story *is* true.'

Jarek pushed away his uneaten dinner before standing up and walking to the side of the gazebo overlooking the beach. The sea was sapphire-blue and the silver sand stretched into the distance. He wanted to run along the water's edge and shut his mind to everything but the rhythmic sound of the waves crashing onto the shore.

He had been running for most of his life, he thought.

He heard Holly move as she came to stand

beside him, and his stomach clenched when he caught the drift of her perfume. Lilies, he thought, pure and sweet and yet subtly sensual as Holly was herself.

'Why do you think Asmir might be telling the truth?' she asked quietly.

'Because I went to Vostov to meet him *and I recognised him*,' he said harshly. 'I remembered him from my childhood—before I went to live at the orphanage.'

'My God...' she said in a shaken voice. 'I need to read the letter again. I couldn't take it all in the first time.'

'I'll save you the trouble.' Every word of the letter was imprinted on Jarek's brain. 'You may know that Vostov is a small principality in the Balkans, closely allied to Bosnia Herzegovina. Twenty-five years ago the principality was affected by the Bosnian war when it was invaded by Serbian forces. The commonly held belief is that Prince Goran attempted to take his wife, Princess Isidora, and their children, Prince Jarrett and the infant Princess Eliana, to safety in neighbouring Croatia. But the car they were travelling in crashed on a remote mountain pass and it was believed that the family were all killed.'

Holly nodded.

'But according to Asmir—who says he was Prince Goran's personal assistant—he managed to escape from the car with the two children before the car burst into flames with the other adults still inside. Asmir states that the royal family had been ambushed by the military forces who had invaded Vostov.'

Holly's brow furrowed.

'If I understood the letter correctly, Asmir says he hid the royal children at an orphanage in Sarajevo, where his sister worked. He thought that even if the military leaders who by then were in control of Vostov realised the children were alive, no one would be able to find them. That was why he changed Jarrett and Eliana's names to...'

She trailed off into a stunned silence.

'Jarek and Elin.' Jarek finished her sentence. 'Asmir forged documents stating that the children's surname was Dvorska, which was his mother's maiden name.'

'Do you remember being told to call yourself Jarek instead of Jarrett?'

'I don't remember *any* of the events Asmir described.' Jarek's jaw clenched. 'At least I have no *conscious* memories—but my nightmares make more sense now. I often dream about being in a car that is travelling fast. I can't picture who else is in the car, but I sense they are scared. I hear loud noises—which might be gunfire. I hear screams, but I don't know who is screaming. I think it might be me.'

Jarek thought of the intense fear he felt whenever he climbed into a car, and frustration surged through him.

'I wish I could damn well remember.'

'We can work on recovering your lost memories,' Holly said. 'The fact that you remember Asmir is encouraging, and with intensive therapy I'm hopeful we will uncover your past.'

She put her hand on his arm, and the gentle expression in her eyes made him want to howl like the child he must have once been—before his emotions had been blunted by the struggle to survive the war in Sarajevo and protect his baby sister.

'The timing of the events Asmir mentions fits,' Jarek said heavily. 'The orphanage was bombed and Asmir's sister was killed. When he couldn't find the royal children he assumed they had also died. But by that time my sister and I had been adopted by the Saundersons and taken to live in England. All the records of children who had lived at the orphanage were destroyed when the building caught fire.'

'Why did Asmir send you the letter if he thought you were dead?'

'He explained that for years he had felt guilty that he'd failed to protect the royal children and had told no one his story. But a year ago he saw my photograph in a newspaper and recognised me as the young boy he had smuggled out of Vostov all those years ago.'

'It's incredible...' Holly's eyes were as round as buttons. 'If Asmir's story is true it means that you are...a *prince*.'

Jarek laughed bitterly. '"Incredible" is right. But even if the story is true, I'm no prince. Vostov's National Council asked me to have a DNA test to prove if I am a descendant of the House of Karadjvic.'

'So…did the test show that you *are*, in fact, Prince Jarrett?'

'I declined to have the DNA test.'

Jarek felt Holly's eyes search his face, but he could not bring himself to look at her.

'I don't understand,' she said slowly. 'You have always wanted to uncover your past and the DNA test would be a start. At the moment you don't even know *who* you are.'

He moved restlessly. 'Until Asmir saw my photograph in the newspaper he and everyone else believed that Vostov's royal family were all dead. What good will it do to dig up the past? Prince Jarrett doesn't exist, and Jarek Dvorska is no good. It's *true*,' he said roughly, when Holly shook her head. 'Ralph Saunderson was right when he called me destructive. I was responsible for my adoptive mother's death.'

His voice lowered to a raw growl.

'And maybe I did something else—something so terrible that my mind has blocked out the memories. Frankly, I don't want to know. If a DNA test revealed that I *am* the son of Prince Goran the press would look for skeletons in my past—and perhaps they would find some. The inescapable truth is that I am not good enough to rule Vostov.'

'*Jarek*...'

Holly's voice followed him as he strode down the beach, but he did not look back at her. His mind swirled with half-formed memories and dark shadows, and the compassion in her eyes filled him with a wildness that made him feel dangerously out of control.

He carried on running into the sea and dived beneath the waves, moving powerfully through the water as he swam across the bay, turned around and swam back in the opposite direction. He lost track of how many times he swam back and forth. The breath burned in his chest and his arms ached, but still he pushed himself, trying to exorcise his demons with hard physical exercise.

But even after he was exhausted his body still ached for Holly. She had followed him down the beach, and each time he'd swum across the bay he had seen her sitting on a rock, watching him. He had the strange feeling that she was guarding him, and the thought made him feel hollow inside.

The sun was low in the sky when he swam back to the shore and walked up the beach to the outside shower. He rinsed the sea water from his skin before heading towards Holly.

He hunkered down in front of her and stared into her big brown eyes. 'I don't need a guardian angel,' he said roughly.

'Listen to me,' she said fiercely. 'You are a good and honourable man. I truly believe that. I did some research about your charity work, and the huge amount of money you have raised for Lorna's Gift actually changes the lives of children who live in orphanages as you once did.'

Her belief in him scraped on emotions that had been buried deep inside Jarek since he was six years old and had walked into that forbidding institution for homeless children in Sarajevo. For the first few nights he had cried because he missed his parents, but he'd quickly learned that crying earned him a beating and he had never cried again—not even at Mama's funeral, even though he had felt as if his heart had been ripped from his chest.

He looked away from Holly, afraid that she would see too much—the part of himself that he'd kept hidden behind his carefully cultivated playboy image. 'I'm no hero,' he muttered.

'You protected your little sister in a war when you were just a child yourself. I think that's pretty heroic,' she said firmly. 'Jarek, you *have* to have the DNA test and accept your destiny. For what it's worth, I think you would be a great prince.'

'Come with me. I want to show you something.'

He stood up and held out his hand to pull her to her feet. Her hand felt soft in his and he linked his fingers with hers as they walked along the beach.

'Where are we going?'

'You'll see.'

He led her around the headland and onto a small, secluded beach surrounded by palm trees. There was a double sun lounger on the sand and he sat down on it, patted the space beside him.

'Take a seat and watch the show,' he invited, pointing to the horizon, where the sun was a huge orange ball that appeared to be sinking slowly into the sea.

The sky was streaked in hues of pink and red

that were reflected on the surface of the ocean. And as the fiery ball sank lower the entire beach was bathed in gold and the fronded leaves of the palm trees were silhouetted against the setting sun.

'How incredibly beautiful...' Holly murmured.

'Yes.'

But Jarek did not glance at the sunset. He only had eyes for her, and the heat inside him blazed like a wildfire—fierce and uncontrollable.

She turned to look at him and he heard her catch her breath when he removed the clasp that secured the knot on top of her head, so that her hair fell like a curtain of silk around her shoulders. She whispered his name and it was the sweetest sound he had ever heard. A siren's song that he could no longer resist.

He had spent three weeks on a paradise island feeling as miserable as sin. He'd missed her soft smile and her sharp wit. And if he did not make her his soon he thought he might die.

Her eyes widened when he leaned towards her, and he felt a quiver run through her as he brushed his lips over hers. She tasted divine, and what little restraint he had left cracked when she opened her mouth to him with a willingness that drove him over the edge.

With a low growl he hauled her into his arms and slid one hand to her nape, to angle her head so that he could kiss her deeply, hungrily. And somewhere in Jarek's mind was the thought that he had come home.

CHAPTER NINE

JUST ONE KISS, Holly promised herself. What harm could there be in one kiss?

The raw emotion in Jarek's voice when he had told her that he remembered Asmir from his early childhood had swept away her defences against him. Asmir's story that Jarek was in fact Prince Jarrett, heir to the throne of Vostov, was almost too astounding to be believable. But if a DNA test proved it to be true then Jarek would be desperate to regain his lost memories about his parents, and he would need her help in the form of therapy sessions.

Holly was aware that it was vital to set boundaries between a psychotherapist and her client. In fact, before she'd left Austria, she had explained to Professor Heppel that her relationship with Jarek had become personal, and she had taken unpaid leave from the Frieden Clinic in order to visit him in the Seychelles. Even so, she knew she should not be allowing Jarek to draw her into his arms and hold her so close that she could feel the hard thud of his heart beneath the hand that she had placed on his chest, intending to push him away.

But he filled her senses, and she could not resist sliding her hands to his shoulders, stroking her fingers over his satiny skin before moving them up to trace across his rough jaw. And all the while his mouth was fused to hers. And he pushed his tongue between her lips as he deepened the kiss so that it became intensely erotic.

She kissed him back because she could not help herself. Because she had missed him the same way that she would miss drawing oxygen into her lungs after he had left the clinic in Austria. When he lay back on the sun lounger and pulled her down on top of him she pressed herself against his hard body and felt a quiver of feminine satisfaction at the feral sound he made.

He took his mouth from hers, and she should have seized that moment to end the madness and lift herself off him. But he trailed his lips down her throat and lower, to the valley between her breasts, and it was then that Holly discovered he had untied the wraparound dress. He pushed the edges of the dress aside, and when he smoothed his hand over her stomach she burned at his touch and every sensible thought flew from her head, leaving her mindless with desire.

In a fluid movement Jarek reversed their positions and flipped her over, so that she was lying beneath him. She ran her fingers through his silky hair and then cradled his face in her hands and kissed him with a hunger that she had never felt for any other man. He had fascinated her from the start, and she was helpless to deny her desire for him when he tightened his arms around her as if he never wanted to let her go.

The soft shadows of the gathering dusk stole around them, enclosing them in their private world, and Holly simply surrendered to the thunder of her heart and the increasing urgency of Jarek's passion. He pulled her bra cup aside and gave a husky laugh when he flicked his tongue across the hard peak of her nipple and heard her catch her breath.

A flame shot down from her breasts to the molten place between her legs and she forgot who she was—forgot that her body was flawed. Jarek used his hands and his mouth to caress her with such artistry, such reverence, that she forgot everything but the heavy pulse of her need that was centred *right there*, where his hand rested on the lacy panel of her knickers.

She lifted her hips towards him when he pressed his palm down hard, and gave a startled cry as the tight band of need inside her snapped and her body shuddered with the intense pleasure he had created simply with his touch.

'Holly...' Her name was a raw growl and his eyes glittered with a feral hunger that belatedly awoke her to the realisation of where this was leading.

'Jarek—' she began, but her voice was smothered when he captured her mouth once more and kissed her with a desperation that tugged on her heart.

She wanted him more than she had ever wanted anything in her life, and the stark look on his face warned her that he was barely holding on to his control.

He rose up onto his knees, and yanked down the zip on his shorts. 'I have to have you,' he said hoarsely. 'I can't wait, angel-face. You're driving me out of my mind.'

With one hand he began to tug her knickers down, and he used his other hand to free himself from his shorts.

Until that moment Holly had told herself that this time it would be all right. She was so turned on that surely her body would allow Jarek to penetrate her. But one look at the hard length of his erection brought her crashing back to reality. For her, having sex had to be a gradual process. If she rushed it would be bound to end in disappointment for Jarek and embarrassment for her.

He stood up to pull off his shorts and kick them away. Truly he was a work of art, his muscle-hard body as beautiful as any marble figure sculpted by Michelangelo. But Jarek wasn't made of stone. He was a hot-blooded male in his prime, and when he moved purposefully towards Holly it broke her heart to know she had to deny them both the satisfaction of the desire that burned like a white-hot flame between them.

'No!' she said frantically, holding out her hand to stop him lowering himself down onto her.

Taking advantage of his stunned expression,

she rolled off the sun lounger and pulled her underwear back into place. Her hands shook as she refastened her dress.

'No?' There was disbelief in his voice. His eyes narrowed and she sensed he was struggling to control his angry frustration. 'What *is* this, Holly? An attempt to pay me back for rejecting you?'

She swallowed. 'I'm allowed to change my mind.'

'Of course.' His ice-blue eyes glimmered. 'But I'm curious to know *why*, exactly. You wanted me.' He swore, and then said with heavy self-derision, 'I've had enough experience of women to be able to tell if you were faking it.'

His casual reference to the fact that he had slept with countless women felt a knife in her heart. She was sure that none of his beautiful mistresses would have had an imperfect body like hers.

'We can't. I... I can't. I'm sorry,' she said in a choked voice, before she whirled away from him and tore across the beach.

Dusk fell quickly in the Seychelles, and the path up to the house was illuminated by fairy lights that glowed as bright as fireflies. Holly ran inside and up the stairs to her bedroom, and after locking the door she curled up on the bed and wept tears of frustration.

On the beach she simply hadn't felt confident that she would be able to make love with Jarek, or that he would want her when he discovered she had a medical condition which meant spontaneous sex was a problem for her.

'Holly, are you all right?'

Jarek's voice sounded through the door, and the doorknob rattled as he tried to turn it.

'Will you let me in? We need to talk.'

'There's nothing to say.' She sniffed. 'Stop harassing me.'

She heard him sigh. 'What happened, angelface? You were with me all the way.'

She swallowed a hiccup. 'You think I led you on deliberately?'

'No, I don't. I said a stupid thing in the heat of the moment, but I know you're not a sexual tease.' His voice deepened. 'I *know* you, Holly. I guess you called a halt because maybe you're not on the pill, and you were right to be concerned that we were about to have unprotected sex. I promise you I have never been careless about contraception before,' he said gruffly.

She gulped. Jarek had no idea that she would never have to worry about an unplanned pregnancy. 'It wasn't that. You...you don't know me at all.'

'Are you *crying*?'

The doorknob rattled again and she heard him swear.

'Let me in.'

'Go away—*please*.' Her voice trembled. 'Just leave me alone.'

After a few minutes she heard his footsteps move away down the corridor. Holly didn't know how long she lay there, feeling sorry for herself, but after a while she decided she might as well go to bed and try to sleep, aware that in the morning she would have to face Jarek and somehow try to re-establish her role as his therapist.

She took off the badly creased silk dress and hung it up. Then realised the brushed cotton pyjamas she wore in Austria would be too hot here in the Seychelles, where the temperature at night only dropped a couple of degrees from the searing heat of the day.

Searching through a drawer for a T-shirt to wear in bed, she found the shirt Jarek had lent her when they had been stranded for the night in the mountain hut. She had packed the shirt so that she could return it to him, but it was the nearest she was going to get to sleeping in his arms, she thought as she slipped the shirt on and hugged it around her.

A noise from over by the sliding glass doors made her swing round, and her heart crashed against her ribs as she watched Jarek climb over the rail and drop down onto the balcony outside her bedroom.

'Are you *crazy*?' she demanded. 'It must be a ten-foot drop at least down to the ground. If you'd fallen you might have broken your neck.'

He ignored her protest and strode across the room, catching hold of her shoulders before she could back away from him. 'Why were you crying? Did I do something to hurt you or offend you?'

'No, of course not.'

'Then why did you run off like that?'

She looked away from his piercing blue eyes

and shrugged. 'Is your ego so big that you find it hard to accept I didn't want to have sex with you?'

He spread his fingers wide on her shoulders and drew her closer to him. 'It has nothing to do with my ego. I *know* you are as hungry for me as I am for you.'

Oddly, considering his words, there was none of the old arrogance in his voice, and he spoke in a low, intense way—as if his emotions were on a knife-edge.

'If I demand that you give me back my shirt right here and now, I'm certain your body won't lie. Shall I put my theory to the test, Holly?' he said softly.

She swallowed when he unfastened a button on the shirt, and then another. The hard gleam in his eyes told her it was not by accident that his knuckles brushed over the upper slopes of her breasts. She felt her nipples become tight and hot and she was powerless to prevent her body from betraying her.

'Say it,' he muttered, and there was something strangely vulnerable in his rough voice. 'You are the most honest person I know. Tell me the truth, Holly.'

She put her hand over his to stop him unbuttoning the shirt any lower, and gave a defeated sigh. 'All right, yes. I wanted to make love with you on the beach. But I couldn't. I just *couldn't*—not easily. Can we leave it at that?' she whispered.

He moved his hands up from her shoulders and cradled her face in his palms. When he spoke, the unexpected tenderness in his voice brought more tears to her eyes.

'I have stripped my soul bare to you, angel-face. You know every one of my deepest, darkest secrets except for the ones I don't even know myself.' He rubbed his thumb-pad over the trembling of her mouth. 'I would never betray your trust in me, just as I know *here*—' he thumped his fist over his heart '—that you would die rather than reveal something told to you in confidence.'

Jarek's faith in her was humbling, and it made her want to cry even more.

Perhaps he could tell from the way her shoulders drooped that all the fight had gone out of her, because he scooped her up in his arms as easily as he had on the mountain after she had been injured in the avalanche and carried her over to the sofa. He sat down and settled her on his lap—as if she were a child in need of comfort instead of a highly qualified professional woman of thirty-one, Holly thought ruefully.

Before he had climbed up to her room he'd changed into jeans and a black T-shirt that clung to his muscular chest and felt soft against her cheek when she rested her head on his shoulder. She felt drained after her storm of emotions. Jarek stroked her hair, and her sense of being comforted and cared for by him was dangerously beguiling.

After a moment she began to speak. 'I have a rare syndrome which means that I was born with a gynaecological abnormality. As a teenager I had to have surgery which would enable me to have sex when I was an adult, and I was also advised by the doctor to use dilators regularly.'

Holly tensed as she waited for Jarek's reaction. In the past, when she had told a couple of boyfriends about her condition, they had reacted with varying degrees of shock. Their main concern had been that her imperfection might affect their enjoyment of sex with her. In each case she had decided not to take the relationship any further.

'That must have a tough experience to go

through,' Jarek said, with no hint of shock or horror in his voice. 'Puberty can be a difficult time anyway.'

She nodded. 'I was fifteen when I was diagnosed, and I found it horribly embarrassing to have to discuss very personal details about my body with medical staff. I couldn't talk to my parents about my feelings, but inside I felt I was a freak and a failure as a woman.'

She was embarrassed, telling Jarek such intimate things about herself, but when she attempted to slide off his lap he tightened his arm around her.

'It was even worse when I started modelling,' she continued after a moment. 'Men desired me for the way I looked, but I knew I hid a shameful secret.'

'Why shameful?' he murmured. 'It's not your fault that you were born with a medical condition.' He continued to stroke her hair gently. 'Was the surgery you underwent to enable you to have sex successful?'

'Yes, but since my last relationship ended over a year ago I haven't had sex, I have used the dilators, but not as often as I should have done.'

'Did the relationship end because of your condition?'

'It was a factor,' Holly admitted.

In fact, when she'd first met Stuart she hadn't explained about her MRKH because she had used her dilators regularly. Sex with him had been uneventful—*and unexciting*, a little voice in her mind whispered. Stuart had finished with her after she had told him she was infertile, but there was no reason to explain that to Jarek.

'Were you in love with your ex?' Jarek frowned. 'I assume you must have been, as you've remained single and celibate for a year since your relationship finished.'

She hesitated. 'I believed that Stuart and I had a future together. I haven't dated anyone else because...' She halted, feeling utterly miserable.

It was all hopeless. She had no idea why she was telling Jarek so much about herself. How could he possibly understand? He probably regretted risking serious injury by climbing up to her balcony like a latter-day Romeo, only to discover that his Juliet was a dud.

His brows lifted. 'Because?'

'I can have sex, just the same as any other

woman,' Holly burst out defensively. 'But it takes time for my body to be ready and most guys are too impatient.'

She stared at him—at the hard, beautiful face that made her heart twist. He was a golden, gorgeous playboy who could have any woman he wanted.

'Truthfully,' she whispered, 'what man would want to make love to me?'

'*This* man,' Jarek said softly.

He lifted his hand and brushed the tears from her cheeks. Holly turned her head away, afraid she would see pity in his eyes that would make her feel worse. But he slipped his fingers beneath her chin and steered her gaze back towards him, and the fierce gleam in his eyes set her foolish heart pounding.

'I told you the truth when I said you were driving me out of my mind, and nothing you have said has lessened my desire for you.'

He stared into her eyes with an intensity that made her tremble.

'I wanted you the minute I set eyes on you in Austria. You blew me away then and you blow me away now. The only difference now is that I know your beauty is not just skin-deep. You are brave and honest, compassionate and infuriatingly stubborn.' Jarek's mouth crooked. 'You are also the sexiest psychologist I've ever known.'

Despite everything, Holly melted at his smile. 'Have you known *many* psychologists, then?' she murmured.

'Only you, angel-face.' He still smiled, but his tone had become serious. 'I would like to make love with you—but this isn't about me...it's about what *you* want.'

'I want you,' she whispered. 'But I've told you... I have to take things slowly...you might get bored.'

Jarek stroked his fingers through her hair, but it no longer felt as if he was comforting her when he slid his hand to her nape and gave a gentle tug to angle her face towards his so that his mouth was a whisper away from hers.

'I promise you that neither of us will be bored,' he said softly. 'Forget those guys who were impatient, and your ex-boyfriend who is clearly a jerk. Your body is beautiful and unique to you, and if it takes a little time for you to become fully aroused and ready to make love what does it matter? We can take as long as we like. Anticipation adds another dimension to the overall pleasure,' he murmured, his voice very deep and very soft, like the caress of plush velvet across her skin.

Holly gave a low moan when Jarek finally claimed her mouth and kissed her with a bone-shaking sensuality that dispelled any doubts she might have had that he genuinely desired her. But she still couldn't relax, and he must have sensed her tension because he lifted his mouth from hers and cradled her cheek in his hand.

'I give you my word that I won't try to rush you before you feel ready.' He trailed his lips down her throat to the sensitive hollow at its base and murmured, 'The route to sexual pleasure has many pathways that we can explore.'

Holly felt like a teenager on a first date. She had been certain that Jarek would reject her, but he had promised to be patient. Her heart was thumping with a mixture of nerves and antici-pation and she needed a few minutes to herself.

'I… I need to go to the bathroom.'

He lifted her off his lap and stood up, bending his head to drop a brief, hard kiss on her lips that left her wanting much more.

He grinned at her obvious disappointment when he took his mouth from hers. 'All in good time, angel-face,' he promised, in a husky growl that caused heat to unfurl in the pit of her stomach.

Five minutes later Holly was tempted to call through the bathroom door and tell Jarek she had changed her mind and did *not* want to make love with him. Except that she would be lying, she admitted to herself. Her lips were still tingling from his kiss and the heaviness in her breasts coiled all the way down to the hot, molten core of her.

She caught sight of herself in the mirror and grimaced when she saw that her eyes were huge and dark, with enlarged pupils. There was a bloom of heat on her cheeks and the hard points of her nipples were clearly visible, jutting beneath the shirt she had borrowed from Jarek.

Was it love or lust that was responsible for her accelerated heart-rate and quickened breathing? She didn't know, and at that moment she did not care. Jarek had insisted that the medical condition she had been born with made no difference to his desire for her. She wanted to believe him, but she had spent the past five minutes in the bathroom to give him a chance to leave her bedroom. She wouldn't blame him if he decided that having sex with her sounded like too much trouble.

But when she opened the bathroom door and saw him sprawled on her bed, naked save for a pair of black briefs, she felt a flash of relief. Simultaneously her stomach tied itself into a knot.

He was diabolically handsome, she thought. Although thinking was difficult when she was fixated on his magnificent body—all that lean, golden hardness, and the sheer perfection of finely honed muscles. All that untamed blond hair that he flicked back from his face with a careless gesture, and those brilliant blue eyes that trapped her gaze from across the room and gleamed with a hunger that was too raw and intense for it not to be real.

'We can make love in the doorway if you like,' he murmured as she clung to the doorframe for support, 'but we will be more comfortable on the bed. Why don't you come over here?'

She licked her dry lips and fought the urge to lock herself back in the bathroom. Jarek was leaning against the pillows, watching her from beneath heavy lids. With a flare of misery Holly wondered how many times he had played out this

very scene: him sprawled on a bed like an indolent sultan, waiting for his mistress—probably
blonde and definitely beautiful—to join him on
the silk sheets.

She gave herself a mental shake as she walked
towards the bed. It wasn't as though she was a
virgin, but she only had fairly limited sexual experience, and she was afraid that Jarek would
find her disappointing.

'Do you trust me, Holly?'

'Yes,' she said, without hesitation. He had saved
her life on the mountain and she knew that physically she was safe with him—although her heart
was a different matter.

'Good,' he said softly. 'Before we begin you
have to agree to two rules. Rule number one—
and the most important—you must tell me if anything we do causes you discomfort and we will
stop immediately. Secondly...' His smile was a
wicked promise that made Holly's legs tremble
beneath her. 'You have to agree to do whatever
I tell you.' When she opened her mouth to argue
he reminded her gently, 'You said you trust me.'

'I do,' she whispered.

'In that case I want you to return my shirt to me.'

'Now?'

Her heart missed a beat when he nodded.

She stared at him, lounging there against the pillows as if he was her lord and she was a serving wench bound to do her master's bidding. For the first time since she had fled from the beach in shame Holly's chin came up and she stopped feeling crushed. If Jarek wanted her to perform a striptease she would damn well give him a performance that would bring him to his knees!

Keeping her eyes focused on him, she lifted her hands and opened the top button of the shirt, and then slowly worked her way down, sliding the buttons out of their buttonholes. She pushed the heavy swathe of her hair back from her face and the action caused the half-open shirt to slip off one shoulder.

Jarek's eyes glittered and he no longer looked relaxed. The idea that *she* was the cause of his tension delighted Holly, and she unfastened the rest of the buttons without taking her gaze from his. She let the shirt slip from her shoulders— slowly, slowly, inch by tantalising inch—baring her breasts in all their proud, firm glory. Her nipples were flushed rose-red and they were hard... so hard they hurt.

Jarek made a thick sound in his throat. His skin was stretched tight over his sharp cheekbones and there was something predatory about his smile that made Holly think of a wolf—with very sharp teeth. She dropped the shirt and it fell to the floor, leaving her with just the fragile wisp of her lace panties to cover her femininity.

Jarek swallowed audibly. 'You are so beautiful,' he muttered, and she was startled to see dull colour flare on his face. 'See what you do to me, angel-face.'

She could not fail to notice the betraying bulge beneath his briefs, and the evidence of his arousal turned her insides to liquid. He made her feel beautiful and, still holding his gaze, she hooked her fingers in the top of her panties and pulled them down so that they fluttered to the floor.

Jarek growled something that might have been a prayer, and Holly gave a confident smile as she put her hands on her hips while he stared and stared at her naked body.

His breath hissed between his teeth. 'Witch. I *knew* you would be the death of me.'

He did not try to hide his desire for her, and the stark hunger in his eyes made her heart beat as hard as a drum when he held out his hand to her. It was anticipation, not trepidation, that shivered through Holly as she put her hand in Jarek's. He pulled her down onto the bed and stretched out beside her, tracing light circles with his fingertips around her navel before stroking his hand over her stomach.

Fire ignited in her belly and shot lower to between her legs when he ran his fingers over the neatly trimmed vee of dark hair that covered her womanhood. She could feel the molten heat of her arousal, but however much she desired Jarek she could not simply pull him down on top of her and take him inside her.

He must have felt her stiffen because he murmured, 'Holly...angel-face...what's wrong?'

'I *hate* my body. I wish I was normal.'

The words tumbled out of her mouth before she could stop them. The truth that she had denied to herself for years finally revealed. She tried to look away from Jarek, but he cupped her cheek in his hand and stared at her with an indefinable expression in his eyes that caused her heart to clatter.

'Then it is up to me to prove to you that your body is utterly perfect,' he said softly.

He laid his finger across her lips when she made an angry sound of denial.

'It's perfect because it's *you*, Holly, and I would not change a single thing about you. But instead of talking let me *show* you how lovely you truly are.'

He moved so that he was kneeling beside her on the bed, and took both her hands and lifted them behind her head so that her fingers brushed against the bars of the headboard.

'Hold on,' he ordered softly, with a sultry gleam in his eyes that caused butterflies to leap in her stomach. 'We're going to play a game. I'm allowed to touch you wherever I want to, but you're not allowed to touch me.'

'That's not fair—' She caught her breath when he stroked his fingers across the soles of her feet before moving up to her ankles.

'That's the rules, angel-face.'

Jarek continued to skim his fingers up her legs with a light touch that nevertheless felt as if he was branding her skin. Holly tried not to tense when he stroked his fingers over the insides of her thighs, but to her surprise he did not touch her intimately, just moved up to her stomach and then higher so that his hands were just below her breasts. She swallowed and silently urged him to caress her breasts, and her nipples that were tight and hard.

But once again he avoided touching her where she longed to feel his hands and instead trailed his fingers lightly over her arms and shoulders, tracing the line of her collarbone and exploring the sensitive spot behind her ears. And all the while he watched her with his brilliant blue eyes, laughing huskily when he stroked the sides of her breasts but still didn't touch the rosy peaks of her nipples that jutted provocatively and ached for him to roll them between his fingers.

Holly felt as though every centimetre of her body was on fire, and she gave a moan when Jarek smoothed his hands over her thighs once again but made no attempt to touch her *there*, where she was so desperate for him to caress her.

'Please...' she whispered, lifting her hips towards his hands. She felt boneless, more turned on than she had ever felt before, and he had not even caressed her in any sexual way yet.

She realised that he was being true to his word and absolutely would not rush her. His patience as he aroused her body was allowing her to relax and put her trust in him utterly, and she couldn't restrain a gasp of pleasure when finally he bent his head and took her nipple into his mouth. The sensation of him sucking hard on the tender peak before he moved across to her other breast evoked a flood of molten heat at her feminine core.

If he didn't touch her *there* soon she thought she might die, but he ignored her soft plea and moved so that he was lying on his back and she was straddling his legs.

'Now it's your turn to touch me. Remember nowhere is off-limits,' he murmured. 'I'm all yours, angel-face.'

Her heart gave a sharp pang, because she knew he wasn't hers in the way she wanted him to be. But he was hers for this night, and he had given her free rein to explore his body. She would use her hands to imprint his male beauty onto her mind in the same way that a visually impaired person used braille, Holly decided as she ran her fingers over his face, along his sharp cheekbones and down to trace the contours of his sexy mouth.

She caught her breath when he drew her finger into his mouth and sucked. How could such an innocuous action be so erotic?

'It's my turn to touch...you're not allowed to touch *me*,' she complained.

He grinned. 'Ah, but I make up the rules.'

His gentle teasing gave her the confidence to be bold, and it was her turn to laugh when she skimmed her hand over his flat abdomen before tracing her fingers over the front of his briefs. He became instantly and impressively erect.

'I don't think I can be patient for much longer. I want to make love with you, Jarek,' she confessed, in a husky voice that did not sound like her own.

CHAPTER TEN

JAREK DID NOT understand what was happening to him. When Holly had admitted that she hated her body, the shimmer of tears in her eyes and the faint tremble of her mouth had ripped him apart. He'd been impressed by her courage when they had been caught in the avalanche in Austria, but her honesty tonight must have taken a hell of a nerve and he admired her more than ever.

But he was getting in too deep, a voice inside him warned. There were numerous reasons why he should not take his involvement with her any further, and none of them were to do with the rare syndrome she had been born with, and which he sensed affected her emotionally even more than physically.

When she had stripped for him, and teased him by taking her time to reveal her gorgeous body, he'd been so turned on that he'd had to restrain himself from ripping the shirt off her.

He tugged her down so that she was lying next to him and felt a hard kick of desire in his gut as he studied every beautiful inch of her body, from the delicate flush of rose on her cheeks and the darker pink of her nipples that contrasted with the pale cream of her breasts. He moved his gaze lower to the indentation of her waist and the sensual curve of her hips, before coming to rest at the tantalising junction between her soft thighs.

He wanted nothing more than to worship her with his hands and mouth, show her that she was Aphrodite, incomparable, the only woman who made him shake with need. But his needs were unimportant. All that mattered was Holly.

He was shocked by the surge of protectiveness that swept through him. The diagnosis of her medical condition when she was a teenager must have been devastating. It had let to a period of depression, but Holly had sought help from a counsellor and gone on to train as a psychologist and psychotherapist so that she could help other people overcome emotional trauma.

She was nothing short of amazing, Jarek brooded. He wanted to see the shadows in her eyes disappear, and he did not care to dwell on why making her happy was so important to him. He bent his head to her breast and captured her nipple in his mouth, smiling when he heard her soft gasp.

He forgot the tangled web of his life, the possibility that his name was not Jarek Dvorska and the intangible horror of his nightmares that he feared hid the truth about his parents' deaths. He forgot everything and dedicated himself to giving Holly more pleasure than he was sure she'd ever experienced with her crass ex-boyfriend.

The realisation that he hated thinking of her with other men should have set alarm bells ringing, but he shut his ears to everything but the thin cry she made when he sucked hard on her nipple before he moved across to her other breast and flicked his tongue over the taut peak at its centre.

He had assured her that they were in no rush, and he took his time to explore her body and encouraged her to explore his—although when she slipped her hand into his briefs and stretched her fingers around his burgeoning erection he had to stop her while he still had enough self-control.

'We want this to last, angel-face,' he growled, when she tugged his briefs down and ran her hands over his buttocks. 'Remember we're playing by *my* rules and you have to do as I tell you. Open your legs,' he ordered softly, and grinned as a scarlet stain spread across her face. 'If you're hot now, you'll be burning up by the time I've finished,' he promised.'

'You're *so* arrogant,' she choked, sounding appalled, although she allowed him to arrange her to his satisfaction, with a pillow beneath her bottom and her legs hooked over his shoulders.

'I'm so *good*,' he assured her, and proceeded to demonstrate that it was not an idle boast.

He tasted her feminine sweetness and used his tongue with devastating effect on her clitoris before he drew the tiny nub into his mouth and sucked. Holly plunged her fingers into his hair and held on as if she was anchoring herself while she threshed beneath his relentless onslaught. Suddenly she gave a guttural cry, and the sound of it made Jarek's gut twist.

While she was still shaking and trembling in the aftermath of her orgasm he gently ran his finger up and down her opening and slowly eased his smallest finger into her. At the same time he kissed her mouth, slow and deep, until he felt her relax. She released her breath slowly.

'Does that hurt?' he asked her.

'No, it feels good.'

She smiled, and Jarek felt something tug in his chest. His body was aching with the force of his desire, but he was determined to be patient and make sex a good experience for her.

He withdrew his finger and replaced it with his thicker middle finger while he rubbed his thumb pad lightly over her clitoris until Holly trembled.

'How about that? Does it still feel good?' he murmured.

'Yes, *so* good. *Oh...*' She moaned when he swirled his finger inside her. 'Jarek, I'm ready now,' she said, with an urgency in her voice that almost made him come there and then.

'Are you sure? I don't want to hurt you...'

He felt as if he was going to explode—especially when she slid her hand down and clasped his thickened shaft tightly in her hand.'

'You won't hurt me.'

She pushed her hair off her face. Her cheeks were flushed and her eyes were deep, dark pools.

'I want you,' she said fiercely, and Jarek knew then that he was never going to survive.

Holly made him feel things he hadn't believed he was capable of feeling, and she made him wish he was a different man from either of the men he thought he might be—a lost prince without a memory, or a feral boy scarred by his memories of a brutal war.

'I want you, Jarek,' she said again, softly this time, whispering her words against his lips as she cradled his face in her hands and urged him down onto her.

'I left a packet of condoms in my trouser pocket.' He remembered just in time, and kissed away her pout as he lifted himself off her.

There was something in her eyes—a flicker of hesitation…he didn't know what—before she murmured, 'It's okay. I won't fall pregnant. And it's safe. I haven't had a sexual relationship for over a year, and you said you have always been careful to use protection with other women.'

The fact that contraception hadn't entered his mind when he had been about to make love to Holly on the beach was a warning Jarek chose to ignore. He guessed since she had assured him it was safe that she was on the pill, or had protected herself against unwanted pregnancy some other way.

He ached to possess her—and it was not just his body, he realised, aware of a deeper ache in that empty vessel he had assumed was his heart.

He shoved the thought away. There would be a time of reckoning, when undoubtedly he would despise himself for his weakness for this woman with her sweet smile and her innocent belief that there was anything good about him. But for now he could fool himself that maybe she was right. And besides, he wanted her too badly to care about tomorrow.

His hunger for Holly bordered on the obsessional, Jarek acknowledged, but that did not make him forget that what she required from him was patience.

He stretched out on top of her and propped himself up on his forearms to take his weight. Her skin was satin-smooth, and she gave a little shiver when his rough chest hair scraped over her breasts. He laughed softly against her lips before he kissed her mouth, and as their breath mingled he pressed forward so that his hard length was there, at her opening.

'Stop me if it hurts,' he said roughly.

'If you stop I think I'll die,' she muttered. 'Please, Jarek, *now.*'

He eased further forward, entering her slowly to allow her internal muscles time to stretch around him. Her soft moan made him halt, but when he tried to withdraw she wrapped her legs around his back and urged him deeper inside her.

'It's fine...really,' she assured him. 'Actually, it's more than fine.'

She smiled, and that ache in his chest got a whole lot worse. He gathered her close and pushed deeper, taking her with exquisite care, making her his. He set a rhythm, slow at first, increasing in pace when she lifted her hips to meet him.

It couldn't last. He had wanted her for so long—a lifetime, it seemed—and the pressure inside him built with every smooth thrust he made into her. But his concern that it might be too much for her made him restrain his passion as he concentrated on giving Holly pleasure. With each steady stroke he took her higher, and he could tell from her quickened breathing that she was nearing the edge.

'Jarek...' She dug her fingernails into his buttocks and moved sensuously against him, urging him in a husky voice to go faster, deeper.

'I'm trying to be careful,' he muttered, struggling to hold back a surge of rampant need when she wriggled experimentally beneath him.

He felt her smile against his cheek. 'I know, and I love you for it. But I promise you're not hurting me.'

Her words jolted through Jarek. He wondered if she was aware of what she had said. What did *love* have to do with *him*? It was an emotion he viewed with deep mistrust. As for not hurting Holly... He cursed silently, because he knew with grim certainty that he *would* hurt her. It was in his nature. He should never have allowed things to get this far, but now it was too late.

'You can let go,' she whispered.

And then it really was too late for him to maintain any kind of control. The heat inside him became a furnace as he clamped his hands on her hips and his next thrust threw them both into the fire. She arched beneath him and gave a startled cry as her body shook and she convulsed around him. Jarek would have liked to take her high again, but for the first time in his life he was overwhelmed by the wildfire that ripped through him, and with a savage groan he came, hot and hard, and felt the burn of it right down to his soul.

After a few moments he lifted himself off her with a reluctance that worried him. He needed to regroup his thoughts and re-establish his boundaries. That word *love* had thrown him, and he couldn't understand why he was still in bed with her when his common sense told him to get the hell out of her room *and* her life.

But Holly seemed unaware of his inner turmoil and snuggled up to him. For a second Jarek froze. He did not *do* cuddling. So why did he draw her against his side and turn his head to breathe in the fragrance of her hair when she rested her head on his shoulder?

She sighed softly and he tensed, hoping she was not about to declare that she was in love with him, which would embarrass both of them. *Obviously* he hoped she wouldn't do that, he told himself.

'So that's what all the fuss is about,' she murmured. 'I never knew...'

He looked at her questioningly. 'Seriously? That was your first orgasm?' He'd suspected, but hearing her say it filled him with a possessiveness that was downright dangerous.

'First *two* orgasms, as it happens. It's nice to know that the press are right about some things.'

'Like what?'

'Well, you *are* often described in the tabloids as a stud.' She gave him an innocent smile while devilment danced in her eyes. 'Now I have proof that it's true.'

For a few seconds he stared at her, and the tight cords that had been lashed around his heart since the grim days of what should have been his childhood in Sarajevo loosened a fraction. Slowly a grin spread over Jarek's face, and for the first time that he could remember he laughed from deep in his gut—a genuine laugh rather than the sardonic humour he was renowned for on the social circuit of Mayfair, or Monte Carlo, or any of the other places where the rich and bored played.

He had never met a woman who made him

laugh the way Holly did, with her dry wit and her refusal to be impressed by him. He was fascinated by the dimples that appeared at the corners of her mouth when she smiled, but he noted too the faint wariness in her dark eyes, and he realised that her teasing had been to disguise her uncertainty.

'Was it okay for you?' Colour flared on her cheeks. 'I mean…maybe sex is better with other women who don't have my…my problem.'

That was when Jarek knew he was in trouble. When that empty vessel in his chest that had never given even a slight twinge before contracted with pain. He closed his eyes briefly, trying to control emotions that were in free-fall. Her hair felt like silk when he slid his hand around her nape and tilted her face to him.

'It was the *best* with you, angel-face,' he assured her gently. 'So perfect, in fact, that when you are ready I think we will have to do it again.'

'I'm ready now,' she whispered against his mouth.

And Jarek couldn't help himself. He kissed her and the world went up in flames.

* * *

In paradise it was easy for Holly to pretend that the world did not exist. For a whole week she and Jarek had been cocooned from reality on Paradis sur Terre, and in that time they had barely been apart—or out of bed, she thought guiltily.

Making love with him had been a revelation, and under his patient tutelage she had learned that her body was capable of experiencing the most intense and indescribable pleasure. When she had explained that she did not need to use her dilators if she was having sex regularly he'd grinned, and assured her that they must heed medical advice and make love as often as possible.

'I'm following doctor's orders,' he said every time he reached for her in the big bed they shared, or tumbled her down onto the sand and made love to her with fierce passion coupled with exquisite tenderness while the waves running up the shore lapped around them.

And when they weren't consumed by their wild hunger for each other, which seemed to grow stronger every day, they talked.

At the beginning of the week Jarek had flown

by helicopter to Mahe, the largest island in the Seychelles, and at a private clinic had met a representative of Vostov's National Council and given a DNA sample which might prove if he was the sole surviving male member of the House of Karadjvic.

'When will you have the result of the test?' Holly had asked when he had returned to the island, which she now realised really was a hideaway. No one—not even Vostov's Council, and certainly not the media—knew Jarek's exact location.

'It could take as long as two weeks. The standard paternity test which would show if Prince Goran was my father isn't possible because he is dead. A mouth swab is the usual method of collecting a sample. But it is possible to retrieve DNA from items used by a deceased person. Unfortunately the palace in Vostov was ransacked during the war, and most of the royal family's personal possessions were destroyed—which is why there are no photographs of the Prince and Princess and their children,' Jarek said heavily. 'However, a monogramed hairbrush which belonged to Prince Goran is being analysed, and it's hoped that enough DNA can be obtained to carry out a paternity test.'

'It sounds like something out of a spy novel,' Holly had murmured. 'So nothing exists that might trigger your memories of early childhood? That's a pity. Sometimes seeing an object—in your case perhaps a favourite toy—might be a reminder of the past.'

'In my dreams I often see a rocking horse,' Jarek had said slowly. 'But I don't know if it ever existed or if it's something I've imagined.' He'd hesitated. 'Sometimes in the same dream I sense the presence of a woman, although I can't see her. I think she might be my mother.'

Encouraged that Jarek had some vague memories, albeit in his dreams, Holly had planned various strategies which might help him to overcome his amnesia. But at the first session he had paced restlessly around the room and become increasingly frustrated when questions designed to prompt his memory had no effect.

'Why don't you start by telling me about the period of your childhood that you *do* remember, when you were at the orphanage in Sarajevo?' she suggested.

'You don't want to hear about the things I saw there,' he'd growled. 'Let's just say that war isn't pretty.'

'I've never thought it was, but you don't need to protect me,' she'd said gently. 'Not talking about the horrors you witnessed won't make the memories go away. You have to take the first step to unlocking the areas of your mind that you have been hiding from for years.'

He had stared at her for a long time, his jaw clenched, and with a bleakness in his blue eyes that had made her want to wrap her arms around him and take away his pain. But neither of the two distinct sides of their relationship allowed her to comfort him, Holly reminded herself. They were lovers—for now—and she'd had sex with him. She was also here as his private psychotherapist and her role was to listen and try to help him, not to fall ever deeper in love with him.

'All right—you win. I'll bloody well talk,' he'd said harshly. 'But not here.' He'd grabbed her hand and pulled her to her feet. 'If you want to know what it was like in Sarajevo I'll tell you.'

And he had, while they'd walked on the beach. He'd told her how he had been scared and con-

fused when he'd found himself in the orphanage,
with no memories of his life before then. He'd
told her about his nightmares and his illogical
terror of travelling in cars. He had even admitted that 'Tarik' was not a boy he had known at
the orphanage.

'I have no idea why in my nightmares I am
shouting for Tarik, but I'm certain that the name
is linked in some way to my amnesia.'

They had walked and walked on the soft white
sand, with the crystal-clear sea sparkling and the
sun blazing down from an azure sky. On an island called heaven Jarek had told Holly about
hell.

His childhood memories of a war-ravaged city
were the stuff of nightmares, and her heart ached
for the scared, abandoned boy he had been in Sarajevo. It ached even more for the man she had
fallen in love with, who was haunted by the face-
less ghosts from his past.

Finally he had stopped talking, and on the secret beach where she had run from him on her
first night on the island he had drawn her into
his arms and they'd watched the sun turn into a
giant ball of fire that sank slowly into the sea.

Beneath a bejewelled sky of pink and gold he had undressed her, then himself, before he'd lain her down on the sun lounger and worshipped her with his hands and lips, with his mouth on her breasts and at the slick core of her. The velvet dusk had closed around them and the cicadas' song had carried on the warm breeze.

'You can let go now,' Holly had whispered.

And with a groan torn from deep in his chest he had spilled into her and in the sweet aftermath of their passion held her close as if he would never let her go.

Which, of course, was an illusion brought about by her wishful thinking—as Holly kept reminding herself in the following days, when it had felt as though there was only her and Jarek and an island called paradise. One day soon the outside world would intrude on her fantasy that this time with him would last for ever...

The end began on a day towards the end of their second week.

'We'll take the boat out,' Jarek said when they were sitting on the veranda, finishing a very late breakfast after they had spent most of the morning in bed. 'We'll sail around the headland to a cove which is only accessible by boat. You mentioned that you wished you could see turtles, so I asked Rani if they nest on the island. He told me that turtles go to the cove to lay their eggs in the daytime, rather than at night, because the beach is so secluded and safe. With luck we might spot them.'

'That would be lovely.' Holly hesitated. 'I take it you haven't heard from the DNA testing clinic?'

'No.' Jarek frowned. 'But a story has been leaked to the media that "an unnamed male" is undergoing checks that might prove he is the heir to Vostov's throne, and several newspapers are speculating on who it might be. Suggestions include a famous European football player and an American pop star,' he said drily. 'There has also been a poll in Vostov which shows that the majority of the Vostovian people are in favour of restoring a constitutional monarchy if it is proved that Prince Goran's son and heir is alive.'

'How do you feel about that?' she asked quietly.

He ran his hand through his hair and looked tense. 'I don't know what I feel about any of it.

The idea that I could be Prince Jarrett is crazy, and yet—' He broke off and shook his head.

'And yet you see things in your dreams that make you think it could be true?'

'In that case why don't I remember my parents?' he said savagely. 'What horror is my mind trying so desperately to hide from me?'

He was still grim and uncommunicative when they boarded the small sailing dingy and he cast off from the jetty. Holly did not know the first thing about sailing, but Jarek was an expert— as he was at most things and especially sex, she thought as she recalled how wickedly inventive he had been when he had joined her in the shower earlier.

As they sailed around the headland and made for the cove Holly used the camera on her phone to take a few photos of the island. She became aware of a sound that grew louder, and glanced up to see a helicopter flying directly towards them.

Jarek swore. 'Lie down on the floor and hide your face,' he shouted to her. 'They're shooting.'

'What?' She stared at him.

Had the helicopter which was now right above

them reminded Jarek of being in Sarajevo when the city had suffered air strikes? Holly wondered. She moved towards him to reassure him, but lost her balance. And as she lurched backwards on the boat she dropped her phone over the side. It immediately sank beneath the waves.

'Damn it. *Oh!*' She gave a cry as Jarek pushed her down to the floor of the boat.

'They are paparazzi in the helicopter—shooting pictures of us,' he told her grimly.

'Are you sure? No one knows that you are staying on the island, or indeed that you might be a prince. And the paparazzi are certainly not interested in *me*,' she said as she watched the helicopter fly away. 'Maybe they were wildlife photographers, come to film the turtles.'

Jarek made a disbelieving sound and continued to steer the yacht towards the cove.

Although his mood improved, and they spent a pleasant afternoon watching the turtles, the incident was another reminder that his life was about to get a lot more complicated if the result of the DNA test revealed that he *was* a prince, Holly brooded. Where, if anywhere, would she fit into his life once he knew the truth about his identity? she wondered.

When Jarek made love to her so beautifully she could not believe that he felt nothing for her other than desire, or that his hunger for her would fade. But maybe all those countless other women who had fallen for his lazy charm had believed the same thing, she thought bleakly.

Dinner that evening was a quiet affair. Jarek had reverted to being the brooding, unapproachable stranger who had gone to such great lengths to avoid her when they had been at Chalet Soline—a lifetime ago, it seemed. And Holly, who had questioned him endlessly about his past in an attempt to break his amnesia, was too afraid to ask him where their relationship was heading.

She pleaded tiredness and took herself off to bed early, unable to deal with his palpable tension or hide her misery. But she still went to his room and climbed into his bed, which she had shared with him for the past two weeks. Surprisingly, she fell asleep almost instantly—only to be awoken in the dark of the night by Jarek reaching for her and pulling her close until that she felt his hard length press between her thighs.

She went to him with a silent sigh of relief that *this* hadn't changed. His fierce passion matched hers, and the underlying urgency she sensed in his caresses only made their coming together wilder, hotter, and so utterly magical that she pushed her doubts aside and showed him with her body the love that was in her heart.

CHAPTER ELEVEN

'*No!*' JAREK CLAWED his way out of the darkness of his nightmare and jerked his head off the pillows. His breath came in harsh pants, as if he had been running, and he remembered that in his dream he had been running through a forest, stumbling over tree roots, branches whipping across his face.

A man's voice was urging him to run faster. His father's assistant Asmir was ahead of him, holding the baby in his arms. Why wasn't his *mother* holding Eliana? Where were his *majka* and *tata*?

He turned his head to look for his parents and saw their car smashed up against a tree trunk. There was a loud bang and the bright orange glow of flames. Why didn't his parents come?

'Majka...' He started to run back to the burning car, but Asmir grabbed his arm and dragged him deeper into the forest...

Jarek swung his legs over the side of the bed

and glanced at Holly as she stirred. But she did not wake up, and his heart twisted when she rolled into the space in the bed that he had just vacated. In the gossamer glow of dawn she looked like a sleeping angel, with her lovely face serene and her soft lips slightly parted. He would have liked to kiss her awake and tug the sheet from her body, to enjoy her one last time. But he dared not touch her now that he understood his nightmare. Now he knew what he had done.

'You destroy everything that is good,' his adoptive father had told him, and he knew now for certain that Ralph Saunderson had been right.

His phone was blinking, indicating that he had new messages. He pulled on a pair of jeans and walked out onto the balcony to read the email from the DNA testing clinic. Shock ripped through him, even though he had been half expecting to have confirmation that he *was* Prince Jarrett of Vostov.

There was a certain irony in the fact that he had received the result of the test on the same day that his amnesia had lifted, Jarek brooded. He was finally able to remember his parents, and he felt a deep sadness for what had happened to them and to him. He had spent most of his life unaware of his true identity, but now memories flooded his mind of his mother and father, and finally he was able to grieve for them.

His phone pinged constantly with new messages. Social media had gone mad, and he quickly discovered why when he read the news story that was making headlines around the world.

Vostov's Prince: Alive but Elusive! screamed one front page.

Where is Prince Jarrett hiding? asked another paper.

One of the tabloids had a photo of him and Holly on the boat, with the caption *Playboy Prince caught in Secret Tryst with Mystery Brunette.*

Who could have tipped off the press that he was Vostov's missing Prince? It had to be someone who worked at the DNA clinic, or even a member of Vostov's National Council, Jarek thought grimly. This was how his life would be from now on. The paparazzi were already fascinated by his playboy image, but their interest in him and those around him would be relentless now they knew that he was a prince.

He studied the images on his phone. At least Holly's face was obscured in the picture, and she was huddled on the floor of the sailing dingy. But it would only be a matter of time before she was identified, and then the paparazzi would stalk her and dig up every personal detail they could find about her.

He went cold at the thought that journalists might somehow get access to her medical records. Holly would be distraught if it was made public that she had been born with the rare syndrome. Despite his assurances that she was perfect, Jarek knew she struggled with body image issues.

The media machine was merciless, and he would have to move fast to protect her. The only way he'd be able to save her from unwanted press attention would be to make sure that Holly's identity remained a mystery.

He would *not* destroy her too, he vowed grimly as his adoptive father's accusation reverberated in his head. But that meant he must send her away from him and never see her again. He would accept his destiny, as Holly had once told him he must do, but he was aware that his life as a prince would be played out in the full glare of the public and the media spotlight.

A small sound from behind him made him turn his head, and he swallowed when he saw her standing there, wearing his shirt that she had never given back.

'I woke up and you were gone,' she said, her voice softly sleepy and so sexy that he was instantly painfully hard. Her dark eyes searched his face. 'Is everything all right?'

Nothing would ever be right again, but he did not tell her that. He shrugged. 'I've had the result of the DNA test and it proves beyond doubt that I *am* the only remaining male from the House of Karadjvic.'

'So you *are* Prince Jarrett. But in your heart you already knew that,' she murmured, 'because you'd remembered that Asmir worked for your father, Prince Goran.'

'I remember *everything*,' he bit out, and silently cursed himself—because he had not meant to say those words. He certainly did not intend to confide in Holly or confess his sins. Even an angel could not give him absolution.

'That's good,' she said gently. 'The secrets in your past have tormented you for too long.'

'Believe me, there is nothing *good* about my memories.'

She said nothing, and Jarek looked away from the deep pools of her eyes before he drowned in them.

'Tarik wasn't a person—he was a dog. My parents gave me a puppy when my sister was born.'

The words spilled out of him and he was unable to stop them. His grim little story had festered in his subconscious for so long, and in a strange way it was a relief to unburden himself to the one person he trusted absolutely.

'I was jealous of Eliana—Elin, as she is called now. Everyone made a fuss of the new baby, and I...'

He gripped the balcony rail as memories flooded his mind. He hadn't been a nice child, Jarek thought. He remembered feeling angry because his parents had loved the new baby more than him.

'I threw tantrums to gain attention. But then one day there was a puppy in the nursery—a cute little thing. Tarik was *my* dog, my father told me. But I would only be allowed to play with the puppy if I behaved like a young prince should.'

He closed his eyes and saw himself at six years old.

'One night my mother woke me up and told me that we were going on a trip in the car. We had to hurry, she said. But I couldn't find Tarik, and I had a tantrum because I didn't want to leave without the puppy. My father was shouting at my mother to put me in the car.'

He let out a harsh breath.

'I'd never heard my father raise his voice before. My mother said I couldn't waste any more time searching for the dog. I had to be good and get into the car so that we could leave, or something bad would happen.'

He shook his head.

'I had no idea, of course, that Vostov had been invaded and my parents had been tipped off that the military dictatorship planned to ambush and kill the royal family.'

He swung round to face Holly.

'Don't you see?' he said savagely. 'It was *my* fault that my parents died. *My* bad behaviour caused my parents to delay escaping from the palace. Because of me something bad *did* happen—just as my mother had told me it would. My parents were trapped in the car when it exploded. My sister and I only lived because Asmir managed to get us out of the car in time, and then hid us at the orphanage in Sarajevo to protect us from being discovered by the military who ruled Vostov in place of my father.'

He stared at Holly and wondered why she hadn't recoiled from him in horror.

'Ralph Saunderson believed I was responsible for Lorna's death, but my ability to destroy began when I was a child,' he said rawly.

She shook her head. 'You said it yourself. You were a *child*.'

She walked across the balcony and stood in front of him, and the compassion in her eyes stunned Jarek because he knew he did not deserve it.

'Six-year-old boys have tantrums,' she said steadily. 'And an older child will often feel jealous of a new sibling. These things happen in families everywhere, and just because you behaved like a normal six-year-old it does not make you responsible for the atrocity committed against your parents in a time of war.'

He almost believed her. But he heard his mother's voice telling him that something bad would happen if he wasn't good, and he saw the car with his parents inside burst into flames. He heard a shot fired from a gun and saw his adoptive mother fall to the floor, and he listened to Ralph Saunderson telling him he was reckless, destructive.

He tensed when Holly stepped closer to him and breathed in the sweet fragrance of her hair, which gleamed like raw silk in the pale gold light of early morning.

'I wish you could see the man I see,' she said softly. 'You don't destroy people. You saved your sister. You created a charity to help children living in orphanages have better lives.' She hesitated and lifted her eyes to his. 'You saved *me*.'

'It was my fault you were on the mountain when the avalanche struck,' he growled.

'I don't mean then. You didn't reject me when I told you about my medical condition. You were patient, and you helped me to accept my body instead of feeling ashamed that I need to use dilators so that I can have sex.' Soft colour came into her cheeks. 'And you made love to me with such wonderful passion that it's hardly surprising I... I fell in love with you.'

Jarek wanted to believe her. He wanted it so badly that he almost reached for her.

But he stopped himself because he knew the truth. He had been his adoptive father's heir but his parents had loved only his baby sister. Ralph Saunderson had barely tolerated him and his adoptive mother had pitied him. Elin had loved Lorna Saunderson, until he had ruined that for her, and now she loved Cortez.

No one had ever loved *him*, and he could see no reason why that would change—or why he should want it to, he reminded himself. Despite Holly's assurances he knew what he was, that he ruined lives. He was determined not to ruin hers.

'I warned you against falling in love with me,' he drawled, finding it harder that he'd expected to slip into the role he had carved out for himself years ago.

But somehow he needed to find the careless playboy who drank too much and laughed too hard. *God*, he would never laugh again—not the way Holly had made him laugh, with her wicked sense of humour and her warmth that felt like permanent sunshine.

He watched her expression change and become guarded, and the knowledge that she was guarding herself against him felt like a knife in his heart even as he told himself it was what he wanted. It was best for her.

'Could it be that you have ideas about being a princess?' His brows arched. 'You must admit that your timing is off. You tell me you love me ten minutes after learning that I am royal by birth?' he mocked.

She pressed her lips together and Jarek sensed that she would rather die than cry in front of him.

'You don't believe that,' she said, with a quiet certainty that rocked him. 'And, if you care to remember, I told you I love you the first time we slept together.'

He frowned. 'I assumed you said it in the heat of the moment and didn't mean it.'

'I never say things I don't mean. I've told you that I believe you are a good man and that you will be a great sovereign of Vostov. I understand why you are pushing me away, Jarek...'

Her gentle tone ripped him apart.

'But if you shut love out for ever I fear you will find life lonely at the top.'

It killed him to smile the lazy smile that had always come so easily to his lips at parties and meant nothing. But he had to protect her from the danger he knew he was.

'You obviously didn't read fairy tales when you were growing up,' he said, with a laugh that sounded fake to his own ears. '*Every* woman wants a prince, and I don't imagine I'll be lonely for long.'

He turned away from the hurt in her eyes and curled his hands around the balcony rail. The sun was rising over paradise, heralding a new day, but Jarek knew that from this day forward he would never watch the beauty of a sunrise without thinking of Holly.

'It will be better if we are not seen together, so we'll leave the island separately,' he told her. 'The helicopter will take you first and come back for me later today.'

'So this is goodbye?'

He did not hear her bare feet walking across the balcony, and he tensed when she was suddenly standing beside him. She put her hands on either side of his face and the ache inside him grew worse when she reached up and covered his mouth with hers. Somehow he held himself stiffly, and after a moment she ended the kiss and stepped back from him, her cheeks flushed and a betraying shimmer in her eyes.

'Be happy,' she whispered.

Jarek stared at the beach and did not turn to watch her walk away from him. He stood there, frozen, until he heard the helicopter take off, and when he looked up at the sky the sun was so bright that his vision was blurred.

It must be that, for it could not be tears that blinded him, Jarek assured himself. A man with an empty heart could not cry.

The window boxes outside the flat in Greenwich that Holly co-owned with her best friend Kate were ablaze with yellow daffodils. According to Kate, there had been snow in March, while Holly had been abroad, but April had arrived with pale sunshine, and the trees were sporting vibrant green leaves.

'A couple of items of mail arrived for you, but I couldn't forward them to you while you were staying at your secret location,' Kate told her. 'Are you allowed to reveal why you spent a month in Florida? Not that I'm jealous of your gorgeous tan!'

'I can't break a patient's confidentiality, but I can tell you I was giving counselling to a famous golfer who needed to work through some issues,' Holly explained. 'He chose not to check into the Frieden Clinic in Austria, so I stayed with him and his family at a secret location in Florida because he wanted to avoid the press finding out that he was seeing a psychologist.'

She found her unopened mail on the kitchen worktop, next to a pile of old newspapers ready to go into the recycling bin. Although Holly knew it was a form of masochism, she couldn't help herself from reading the numerous headlines about Vostov's return to a constitutional monarchy and its plans for the inauguration of Prince Jarrett. The Vostovian people were delighted to have their royal family back, and there had been many pictures of Princess Eliana, with her impossibly handsome husband Cortez and their two young children, when they had visited the Principality.

Elin was very beautiful, Holly thought as she studied a picture of Jarek's sister. It must have been a great shock to her when she had learned of her royal heritage.

There was much speculation in the press about Prince Jarrett's need to find a bride to be his royal consort. The names of several minor royals and the daughters of aristocratic families across Europe were being mentioned. No doubt Jarek would marry a stunning bride with an impeccable pedigree and they would have beautiful children, Holly thought miserably.

While she had been in Florida she had focused on her job as a way of supressing her heartache, but as she stared at a photo of Jarek it all came hurtling back—his cold rejection and her stupid hope that if she kissed him she would reach the heart that she had glimpsed during those heavenly two weeks when they had been lovers in paradise. Holly went hot at the humiliating memory of how she had thrown herself at him.

She flicked through the pile of mainly junk mail addressed to her and opened a gold envelope, expecting it to contain advertising material.

An embossed card fell out, and she saw that it

was an invitation to the Prince Jarrett's inaugural ball to be held at the royal palace in Vostov on the tenth of April.

The tenth was in two days' time, she realised.

Reading down, she discovered that she should have responded to the invitation a few days ago. At the bottom was a handwritten message, and her heart slammed into her ribs when she saw that it was from Jarek and said simply—*Please come. I need you.*

Twenty-four hours later Holly was following a footman along a corridor on her way to meet Jarek at his private apartment in the palace.

Everything had been a blur from the moment she had called the phone number on the invitation and given her name. A palace official had told her that a car would collect her from her London flat and take her to the airport, where Jarek's private jet would be waiting to bring her to Vostov.

She'd barely had time to pack, let alone question why she had agreed to see him when it was bound to end badly. But he had written on the invitation that he needed her, and like a fool she had rushed to him—again, she thought ruefully.

From the air, Vostov's royal residence had looked like a fairy tale palace, perched on a mountain, surrounded by higher snow-capped peaks and overlooking a gentian-blue lake. Inside, parts of the palace were still undergoing extensive restoration work, following the dark period of Vostovian history when a military dictatorship had imposed rule over the principality and the palace had been left to fall into ruin.

But now it was a new era, with the return of the monarchy, the footman told Holly. Prince Jarrett was already hugely popular, and he had published his plans to turn Vostov into a business hub and tourist venue which would bring wealth to the country.

The footman opened a door and stood aside for Holly to enter an elegant sitting room. Her stomach swooped when she saw Jarek standing in front of the fireplace. *He looked like a prince.* That was her first thought. His blond hair was shorter, although she noticed that he still pushed it off his brow, and for once he was clean-shaven. His face was leaner and even more handsome than the image of him that haunted her dreams.

The suit he wore was exquisitely tailored to

show off his broad shoulders. But it was his eyes that held her attention: brilliant blue, and glittering with an expression she could not define but which made her heart-rate quicken when he crossed the room to stand in front of her.

'You look beautiful,' he rasped, almost as if it hurt his throat to speak.

She saw now he was closer that his skin was drawn tightly over his sharp cheekbones, making his resemblance to a wolf even more marked. She felt his gaze burn through the white silk jersey dress with its deep vee at the front. She had bought it in Florida and it had somehow seemed less revealing in the Sunshine State than it did in a palace. She was conscious of how the material clung to her curves and showed plainly that she wasn't wearing a bra. Jarek's eyes lingered on her breasts and she flushed as she felt her nipples harden.

'Where the bloody hell have you been for a month?' he demanded, making Holly flinch at the whiplash of his voice. 'Professor Heppel at the Frieden Clinic refused to reveal where you were, and your phone number was unavailable.'

'I had to get a new phone because I dropped mine over the side of the boat,' she reminded him.

She wished she could act cool, but she could feel the erratic thud of her pulse at the base of her throat, and with a flash of despair she realised that she would never escape from the spell he had cast over her—and she would never stop wanting him or loving him, a little voice in her head taunted her.

'How are you?' she whispered into the vast ache of tension that filled the room.

'Confused,' he said.

And now his voice did not feel like the sting of a whip. It was a low growl that made her skin prickle with sensual heat.

'You told me you love me, and yet ten minutes later you boarded a helicopter to take you off the island and effectively disappeared from the face of the earth. What kind of love is that?'

Her temper simmered. 'What did you expect me to do after you had made it so very clear that you didn't return my feelings?' she snapped. 'I had made enough of a fool of myself. There seemed no point in prolonging my embarrassment.'

His eyes narrowed on her scarlet face. 'Why did you come to Vostov? I'd given up hope that you would attend my ball when you ignored both the invitations that were sent to you. One went to Chalet Soline in Austria and the other to your London address,' Jarek said roughly.

'I didn't open it until I returned to London from Florida, where I'd been treating a patient. I came because you said you needed me. I assume you meant you needed to see a psychotherapist, and it isn't the first time I've flown across the globe at your command.'

Her eyes flashed at him.

'I definitely did *not* come to Vostov because I hope you will make me a princess,' she said sharply. 'From what I've read in the newspapers you won't have any problem finding a bride to be your consort. You're Europe's most eligible bachelor—I'm sure you haven't been lonely at all.'

Holly looked away from him, hoping he hadn't heard the scratch of jealousy in her voice.

'I've always been alone,' he said quietly. 'Until I met you. The vacancy for my bride is still open, as a matter of fact...' His casual tone was at odds with the intensity of his gaze. 'If you are interested.'

'Jarek—don't.' She couldn't keep it together, and knew the tremble in her voice betrayed her. 'If you asked me here so that you can carry out some kind of refined torture...'

He slipped his hand beneath her chin and tilted her face up so that she was forced to look at him. And what she saw made her catch her breath.

'You told me to be happy,' he said, so grimly that she ached for him. 'And then you left. It felt like I'd been kicked in the gut. The truth was so clear but I had been so blind.'

His beautiful mouth shook and Holly's heart stood still.

'I had never been truly happy before I met you, and I knew as sure as hell that I would never be happy if I let you go.'

'Jarek...' Holly could not stop the tears that blurred her eyes from falling.

'I thought of all the things you had said,' he continued, in that rasp of a voice that was so raw it hurt her to hear it. 'You saw something good in me that nobody else saw and you made me think that I *could* be a better man, that I wasn't stuck for ever with the labels that Ralph Saunderson and others had put on me.'

He lifted his hand to her face and brushed away her tears.

'More importantly, you made me want to be a better man—a man you would be proud of.' He hesitated and stared at her, his expression unguarded and oddly desperate. 'A man you would love as deeply as I love you.'

She was afraid to believe him. 'You don't...'

'How could I *not* fall in love with you, angel-face?' he said softly. 'I thought I could protect you if I sent you away. But I was beyond miserable. And then I remembered you had told me you never say anything you don't mean, and I started thinking that if you *did* love me maybe you were as unhappy as I was.'

Holly's breath caught in her throat when Jarek dropped down onto one knee and reached into his jacket pocket. Through her tears she saw the sparkle of a diamond ring, and then he took her hand in his.

'Holly, my angel, will you marry me and be my wife, my Princess, and the love of my life?'

She shook her head, and her tears fell faster

when the light in his eyes dulled and she saw the abandoned boy he had been in the face of the man she loved but had to let go.

'I can't marry you,' she choked. 'There's something you don't know about me.'

She pulled away from him and ran over to the door, but his voice stopped her.

'You mean the fact that you are unable to have children, don't you?'

'How do you know?' She turned slowly and watched him walk towards her.

'The syndrome you were born with is commonly known as MRKH, am I right?' At her nod, he continued gently, 'I did some research and I guessed you had been diagnosed with the syndrome when you hit puberty but your periods did not start because you were born without a womb.'

'I've come to terms with my infertility,' Holly said huskily. 'But you are a prince and you have to have an heir to continue the royal line.' She swallowed hard. 'I love you with all my heart... maybe I could be your mistress for a while, until you decide that you want to marry and have children.'

Jarek released his breath with obvious relief and his mouth curved into a grin. 'I hope you know that I will never let you forget that you propositioned me,' he murmured as he pulled her into his arms. 'I have already told Vostov's National Council that I intend to marry you, and I have explained that we won't have children. It has been agreed that the royal line will continue through my nephew. Elin's son Harry will be my heir, but if he chooses not to be the next Prince, Vostov will simply be ruled by the National Council after my death.'

'But you *must* want your own child?' she said painfully.

'I want *you*. You're all I'll ever want or need.'

The truth of his words was there for Holly to see in the fierce glitter in his eyes.

'I intend to combine my role as Prince with my work with Lorna's Gift, and I hope you will work with me. Your training as a psychologist will be invaluable to the many children in the world who need support.'

'I don't know what to say,' Holly whispered.

Moments ago the future had seemed hopeless

and bleak, but now the look in Jarek's eyes—the *love*—filled her with a fragile hope.

'Just say yes to the following questions,' he told her, with a touch of his old arrogance that she adored because it was part of him. 'Do you love me?'

'Yes. More than life.'

'Will you marry me and be mine for ever?'

'Yes,' she said tremulously. 'If you will be mine.'

'I have always been yours, angel-face,' Jarek told her as he slipped an exquisite square-cut diamond ring onto her finger. 'I fell in love with you when you stood up in a hot tub, wearing the sexiest swimsuit I've ever seen.'

The heat in his gaze burned its way into Holly's soul so that when he kissed her she melted against him and kissed him back with love, with hope, and with a promise whispered against his lips that her heart was his for ever.

* * * * *

*If you enjoyed Jarek's passionate love story,
don't forget to read his sister Elin's story
in the first part of Chantelle Shaw's
THE SAUNDERSON LEGACY duet*

THE SECRET HE MUST CLAIM

*And also by Chantelle Shaw
ACQUIRED BY HER GREEK BOSS
TRAPPED BY VIALLI'S VOWS
MISTRESS OF HIS REVENGE
MASTER OF HER INNOCENCE
Available now!*